It's Not Right... but It's Okay

Anuj Tiwari is the author of the bestselling books, *Journey of Two Hearts* and *It Had to Be You*. A speaker in many colleges and universities, his stories are based on real-life incidents that he has recorded over the years. With an MBA degree in finance and human resources management, Anuj works in Mumbai as an IT professional and marketing consultant.

To know more about him, visit www.anujtiwariofficial.com or www.facebook.com/anujtiwari.official, or follow him on Twitter @AnujOfficial.

Praise for *It Had to Be You* and *Journey of Two Hearts*

'An inspirational romance.'—*Hindustan Times*
'Myriad shades of romance.'—*Deccan Chronicle*
'Anuj's journey touches every heart that beats.'—*Dainik Jagaran*
'Pearls have come down on paper.'—*Amar Ujala*
'An unforgettable love story.'—*Afternoon*

It's Not Right... but It's Okay

ANUJ TIWARI

RUPA

Published by
Rupa Publications India Pvt. Ltd 2016
7/16, Ansari Road, Daryaganj
New Delhi 110002

Sales Centres:

Allahabad Bengaluru Chennai
Hyderabad Jaipur Kathmandu
Kolkata Mumbai

This is a work of fiction. Names, characters, places and incidents are either the product of the author's imagination or are used fictitiously and any resemblance to any actual person, living or dead, events or locales is entirely coincidental.

ISBN: 978-81-291-3732-6

Seventh impression 2018

10 9 8 7

Printed at Yash Printographics, Noida

To love, life and friendship of the four friends.
To my mother—Kusum, my father—Ashok, my sister—Neeraj
and my forever young Nanu.

Contents

Prologue

It is known that first loves are always about overwhelming emotions. The second tests our maturity. The third, however, is always a compromise.

It's a cold Sunday morning and she is lying in bed, curled up within the confines of her blanket. Though awake, she doesn't want to get out of bed. She wonders what is wrong with her life. She rarely drinks but last night when her friend came over with some vodka, she could not control herself. Eventually, she slept off in her balcony and woke up cold and shivering. Her room feels strange now, strewn with cigarette butts and empty bottles.

The sun is pouring in through the gaps in the curtains. She hasn't slept properly in days, but she manages to get up and clean her room.

The birds are chattering and the morning has begun its many activities, yet everything seems gloomy to her. She tries to divert her mind by finding reasons to help herself get through the sadness, but fails time and again. She goes back to the balcony to get some air and looks into the distance. Thoughts flood her mind. Thoughts she doesn't want to listen to.

Does everyone go through this phase in life or is it just me who is suffering?

When we run away from things, they just seem to haunt us and never really leave.

She begins thinking about the past. There are so many memories, ones which made her happy. Yet the overpowering memories are the ones associated with negative emotions. She thinks of her present, the frustrations which seem to have gripped her life. She is tensed. Her head is aching.

I can have a better future. I can. My past doesn't rule my future.

These are words Arjun has taught her. But somehow, these powerful words wilt in front of her present. Her friends have been supportive of her, asking her to be strong, but she cannot find a reason to go on.

Am I responsible for all that has happened to me? Will this affect my family and friends? I cannot afford to trouble them anymore. I have messed up too many times in the past. I deserve nothing better.

She lights a cigarette and takes a long puff, stubbing it within moments.

It's tough for me, I can't live like this. If I want to survive I need to consult a psychiatrist. Otherwise, it's not worth living.

Life has not been kind to her. She understands this. She looks up and then looks down four floors. She sits softly on the railing and sticks one leg out. Suddenly her cellphone rings. It is Arjun. She ignores the call. She closes her eyes and takes a long breath.

'I am sorry,' she murmurs.

Suddenly she hears a known voice from behind.

'What the heck are you doing?' Charu rushes to be by her side and pulls her inside. 'What do you think you are doing?'

Charu makes her sit on a chair near the balcony and holds her tightly. She bursts into tears within seconds.

'Everything will be fine. We all are with you,' she assures her, before taking her inside the room.

Life is all about perspective. Is it not?

A Suspicious Mother

Arjun has just turned twenty-six and she thinks he has matured quite a bit in the last few years. His sense of humour is something she does not appreciate. In fact, she also does not like the female friends he has and becomes especially uncomfortable with the ones who pamper him. She is, after all, an Indian mother who cares too much and sometimes can be quite possessive. But he is not some playboy. He is a genuine person with whom people like spending time, especially because he is funny. However, for mothers, insecurity remains a constant companion.

Arjun's loving family constantly worries about his marriage. They believe in girls getting married by twenty-one and boys by twenty-five according to the Social Opinion Factor (SOF). He is an eligible bachelor in every way.

Arjun thinks that in life, one's purpose is to make others happy. However, he doesn't have many close friends because he cannot find many people who share his wavelength. Sometimes he wonders if there is a problem with his attitude. His closest friends have assured him it is not. He keeps a positive attitude towards life and is a good listener. He manages his time well. He is well informed and one cannot deny his logic in an argument. He believes that everything happens for a reason; and sometimes these reasons emerge out of our own actions. Sometimes they are good, and sometimes they are bad.

Today he is visiting Bareilly, his hometown, before he heads to a book event in Kolkata. He informs his mom of his whereabouts, in fact he does so even when he is in Mumbai, and she notoriously keeps track of his social media updates on her cellphone. His mom is loving and possessive. His father, like most Indian fathers, follows his mom's lead in life.

Arjun is from a Brahmin family and this family is planning to look for a girl with whom he can spend the rest of his life happily.

They are worried about him because they think he'll take years to choose someone, but in fact, he is really not choosy at all. He does not believe in being selective when finding a life partner. He feels if he keeps in mind a few well thought out life principles, the ideal woman will walk into his life on her own. Moreover, he claims that true love exists and hopes to find love someday.

His views always have a logic to them that cannot be ignored. He believes there is always a right time for everything. One cannot have sex before the age of fourteen because one will not enjoy it. One cannot have babies at the age of eighteen because they're too young to be a good parent. In the same way, one should not get married until one actually feels like getting married.

'You can't be so serious about these issues,' his friends tell him. He simply smiles during those moments.

❧

'So how is the food in Mumbai?' his mom asks him while grating carrots in the kitchen.

Arjun is accustomed to royal treatment at home, including delicious home-cooked meals which lead him to the kitchen, where he spends time talking to his mom.

'I miss you and your food, of course. What do you put in halwa by the way?' he asks while peeling green peas.

'I put nothing special in it, and stop eating while you peel the peas,' she says and softly pats him on his head making him drop the peas back in the bowl.

He feels good when she pats him on his head, it shows on his face.

'I wanted to discuss something with you,' she says, wiping her hands with a kitchen towel.

'Is this about a girl?' he asks, still munching on some peas.

'I am not joking.'

'Yes, my father's boss, say. What happened?'

She grins.

'I feel that you have grown up and you need someone to spend your life with. You live alone in Mumbai and you come home for a week or two after months.'

According to her, if one is a grown up, they cannot live alone.

'Are all mothers playing a big role in raising the Indian population?' He laughs while questioning her. 'Mom, I just turned twenty-six in November, and I don't want to marry till the time I fall for someone.'

Arjun understands that his mom wants to keep a check on the mischievous life he has in Mumbai.

'I am just asking you to find a well-educated girl for yourself and that too after your sister's marriage. I am not saying this on the spur of the moment. You live alone in Mumbai, so far from us. So at least there should be a girl who can take care of you and manage things for you. I am getting old, you know,' she says as she opens the fridge and takes out a packet of cashew.

'Mom, I will marry a girl not an air hostess or someone who can travel with me.' He holds her from the back. 'And I really don't want an arranged marriage.'

His mom's frown is enough to show that she is not in favour of love marriage.

Every secret conversation between mom and son takes place in the kitchen. It's a practice which has been going on since Arjun was a child. He always sits on the slab and helps her prepare the salad or chop chillies, or sometimes he washes the rice grains before cooking. Times have changed and he now debates over topics like love and arranged marriage with her.

'Your views are absolutely correct and I respect them but times have changed. How can someone marry without even knowing the person?' he asks.

'Hmm...' is all she says in response.

Her Hmm does not satisfy him and he continues to convince her of the validity of a love marriage.

'Listen, marriage is not just about making your sex life...'

'What?' She suddenly turns towards him leaving everything aside.

'I mean, marriage is not just about making one's affair official on a legal document. It involves a lot more responsibilities. Moreover, to tie two families with such high expectations and that too for a lifetime is demanding. Look at my father.'

She pretends to work but intently listens to everything he has to say, all the while choosing not to reply.

'At what time do you have to leave for Kolkata tomorrow, Arjun?' she asks as she walks out of the kitchen. Before he can even reply, she says, 'Dinner is ready. Call everyone, Arjun.'

'Mom, what happened?' he asks, conscious of the change in her behaviour. 'Are you making this face because I leave tomorrow or because I am debating with you?' he asks again, following her from the hall to the kitchen.

'What if I say both?' she says.

This happens every time. Whenever Arjun is about to return, his mom becomes emotional.

'Mom, it's been eight years that I have been away from home, and you still become emotional every time I leave.' Arjun tries to console her.

She ignores him but Arjun is sure that she is going to cry as the time of his departure comes closer.

'Don't worry, I won't run away,' he says, trying to pacify her as he knows it's bothering her but she cannot bring herself to talk about it.

'But be careful about our status in society. You live there and you must be meeting many girls, but be careful because I won't support you at every step.' She puts a chapati on his plate while waiting for others to join them.

'What if I fall in love with someone? And what if that someone falls for me?'

Arjun holds her shoulders while she keeps the plates on the table for others. 'Mom, listen, please. I promise, I won't hurt you by making commitments to anyone without your permission. Can you please smile now? Please?'

'Okay, now sit and have dinner,' she says, turning her back to him.

Arjun knows she has smiled secretly.

'Okay, let's make a deal—my choice, your permission.' Arjun says, as everyone starts gathering at the dining table.

His dad sits on his right and his elder sister Nee sits to the left. Her name is Neeraj, but he calls her Nee because it's the nickname he gave her since he learned to talk. These days, his Nanu is also at home.

'Kusum, why don't you join us as well?' his Nanu asks his mom.

He has just crossed over into his sixties but the older he gets, the more liberal he becomes. This is what Arjun has come to understand. This singular and surprising aspect of his ageing has brought them closer in the last few years.

'You can start. I will join in some time,' his mom replies from kitchen.

That has been her nature for as long as Arjun can remember. To have her meal right at the end after serving everyone. She comes to the hall and pours daal in his bowl, and refills all their glasses with water.

His Nanu had heard the conversation between Arjun and his mom. With his experiences his Nanu weighs in on love and arranged marriages. He feels lucky to have a grandparent who gets better with age, just like fine wine, and who discusses Arjun's life openly without any reservations.

'You should register yourself on matrimonial portals. There are so many options and you can meet someone well suited,' his Nanu says.

'Not a bad option?'

'Yes, try that. You must.'

'Nanu, are you sure you want me to register on a matrimonial portal?' Arjun asks with a smile. He continues, 'There is no need for that. Someone will surely come my way someday. As of now, I need to pack my bag. I have to leave for Kolkata. If I stay here for a few more weeks I'll surely be married to someone by the end of it.'

'By the way, Bong girls are beautiful though they are clever as well,' his Nanu says with a hearty laugh.

'Nanu,' Arjun says, embarrassed.

'Yeah, I know. I have spent nine years of my life there,' his Nanu says, smiling.

'You must concentrate on your work. There is no hurry, okay? And don't listen to him,' his mom says, her anxiety showing on her face.

She continues, 'Well, Anushka is also going to Kolkata with you, right?'

'Yes.'

'And where will she stay?'

'Don't worry, Mom, she's not staying with me. She has relatives in Kolkata,' he teases her.

'Pack your bag and dress appropriately wherever you go.'

'Yes, Ma, I will.'

'By the way, she is not coming. I just got her message.'

'How can she ditch you at the last moment?' his mom fumes, curious as to why Anushka can't make it to Kolkata. 'Anyway, you take care and sleep now. You have an early morning.'

The next day Arjun flies to the city of joy, though he knows he will miss Anushka. They had made plans to meet in the city, but her change of mind has dampened his mood.

Anushka is a friend who has always helped him in his personal and professional life since he was in college. She is from a Punjabi family and stays in Delhi. She was a year senior to him in college. After her engineering, she joined Vccenture Services in Bangalore as a Business Analyst, and a year later Arjun joined the same organization in Mumbai. She got frustrated with her nine to six job and left it to pursue an MBA from IIFT in Delhi.

When Arjun went through a tragic breakup and was in depression, Anushka helped him through the bitter six-month phase. They are like soul siblings. They know almost everything about each other, sometimes more than a friend should. She goes shopping with him whenever he is in Delhi. He shares all his problems with her. He drops her home after nights out in clubs and pubs. She wakes him up early in the morning and then they continue to talk till the evening. They have shared the same glass of drink, even the same bed, but they are just friends. The best of friends.

A Friend I Can Count On

There is an air of excitement as Arjun lands in Kolkata. The afternoon is buzzing with possibilities. He imagines the new faces he will meet, the new stories he will encounter, and the new experiences which will enrich him. Yet the crowds around make him anxious.

He feels he should listen to his mom and get into a relationship. By getting engaged at least someone will be there to pamper him or choose the colour of the shirt he is going to wear or the hairstyle he should keep. However, his mom wants him to get married without getting into an affair or a relationship. Sometimes during these moments he feels alone, but he is courageous enough to deal with it on his own. He is not scared of the future, or of the successes and failures that are headed his way. He has made peace with the possible ups and downs of life.

After a cab ride, a run through some streets and lanes and crossing the tracks of the historical trams of Kolkata, He finally reaches South City Mall at 4.45 p.m. He crosses the central area of the mall and takes the escalators. He enters a quaint bookstore— the venue for the author's meet.

Why don't they keep it in an open area, like at the centre of the mall? Arjun thinks while stepping inside the bookstore. *I think I am not that big yet. I mean, I am not that big an author, but I will be one someday, and then I will interact with my readers in a larger space.*

Everyone settles down as the host announces the commencement of their meet. He takes a sip of water, as his nervousness on meeting new people makes his throat go dry constantly.

A few girls look inside through the glass windows curiously. He remembers what his Nanu said—Bong girls are beautiful but they are modern and clever too.

Well, it's time for me to see how clever these Bong girls are. I hope I have an interesting discussion with them.

Arjun is not tall but has broad shoulders and the blue blazer he has worn falls perfectly on his frame. His dark hair and solemn brow give him a look of being introspective, observant and analytical, while his boyish grin makes him approachable. He wears square-framed spectacles which keep sliding down his small nose. He has a light beard on his face which gives him that rugged look. His natural charm and friendly disposition make it easier for people to ask him questions and get to know him better.

I am the best. I am the best. I am the best.

He is energized and in high spirits and keeps repeating these lines to himself.

He has been using this trick since his college days when he wasn't sure of what to say during a presentation.

Arjun talks about relationships, friendship and life. He reads a few chapters from his book too. The session becomes interactive and interesting with time. It takes forty-five minutes to end the event which is sooner than he expected. Now, it is time to answer some questions from the audience.

Someone from the crowd asks, 'What do you think about Indian families and their opinions about love and arranged marriage?'

Arjun smiles and remembers the discussion he had last night with his family. He answers after taking some time. 'I'm looking for the answer myself. I am a victim of the same type of family.'

Everyone starts laughing.

He doesn't take much time getting comfortable with the audience and soon everyone is listening to him with rapt attention. Even the host is giggling standing near him.

'You have a good sense of humour,' the host mutters into Arjun's ears as he takes another sip before requesting for the last question of the session.

'Credit goes to my family,' he says with a funny expression.

Both of them laugh. Arjun realizes that he has answered almost every question well, barring a few.

'Last question, Arjun,' someone says from the back. 'What do you think about true love in today's world? Does it really exist or is it just a term which is used in books and never found in hearts.'

Arjun follows the voice in order to find who has asked this question. At the extreme end he spots the face and smiles before answering her question.

She gets up and repeats her question.

'Hi, this is Anushka. Can you tell us something about the similarity between the love you have experienced in your own life and the one you write about in your books?

Arjun is surprised but does not let it appear on his face. He pretends she is an unknown face.

'Love still exists in hearts, not in books. Books exist to make them live forever. And to answer your question specifically, there is nothing called true or fake love or book-ish love for me. It's completely about how we feel about someone, and I believe if you love someone you love them forever. So, whatever I have experienced in life I have tried to translate it in my books. I feel lucky to be able to convey them in words. Well, I just want to say, if we have a past that we aren't particularly proud of, it doesn't mean that we can't have a promising future. To those of us who have a great present, let's cherish these moments and look forward to a wonderful future.'

The session gets over in the next few minutes and Arjun desperately looks for Anushka in the crowd.

He is reminded of the first time he met her. It was when she was gorging on a hot dog in a college cafeteria, and he had accidentally laughed at her loudly. Though he had to pay a price for it later, it was all worth it because he got a friend like her.

'Are you looking for me, Arjun?'

He turns back and notices the wide stunning smile and the adorable dimples that have become more prominent over the last couple of years. Anushka looks beautiful. The innocent yet playful expression in her eyes; the pronounced cheekbones and her long eye lashes; her shiny long honey-coloured hair, red luscious lips, a heart-shaped face and her luminous black eyes; her understated beauty is enough to make many men go weak in their knees. Arjun smiles and gives her a hug.

'If you have come here just for me, it is the nicest surprise anyone has ever given me. Though I doubt that you had it in mind to surprise me,' he says.

He takes out a chocolate from the inner pocket of his blazer. He usually carries one, especially if he's going for an event.

'I know surprising people is not your thing. So are you going out of your way just to show that you care for me?' He gives her the chocolate. 'This is for you. And why don't you start wearing blue lenses. You's look smoking hot in them.'

'Shut up. I look pretty anyway. By the way, since when did you start keeping chocolates in your pocket? Is there someone special in your life?' she asks.

'These help when people ask tough questions and I can't answer them,' he says, taking out a piece of chocolate and popping it into his mouth.

They both have a hearty laugh.

'So you didn't tell me yet. What is the reason you are in Kolkata? You were supposed to come with me, right?'

'Yes, I am on vacations with family. I have come with my chacha and chachi. Just to spend time with my family. Moreover, I was following your updates on Facebook, so thought it would be fun to give you a surprise. I extended my stay here by one more day and have come to meet you. By the way that was a nice line you read earlier—if we have a past that we aren't particularly proud of, it doesn't mean that we can't have a promising future. To those of us who have a great present, let's cherish these moments and look forward to a wonderful future. That's so true. You have learnt so many things from me in the last couple of years.'

'Yes, you are responsible for my good and bad habits.' Arjun smiles looking at her.

'Oh please, not your bad ones,' she says, still eating the piece of chocolate.

Sometimes, you just need a shoulder to cry on or someone to

laugh with, and that is what best friends are for. Anushka has always been that friend to Arjun.

'So how's Aunty?' Arjun asks.

They both come out of the bookstore and walk towards Coffee World.

'Mom is fine.'

'And how's Angira. I got your message but didn't reply because I wanted to talk about it over the phone instead of doing it over messages. Now that you are here, we should talk.'

Karaoke Night

Angira is Anuhska's younger sister. She always wanted to start a venture of her own but she was confused. Left with no other choice, she joined Delhi College of Engineering. She stayed in the hostel with her friends, which was a big transition from living with her parents. She became a gutsy, outgoing girl. After spending four years in college, she wants to take the risk of studying fashion designing in Mumbai in order to start her own business. She believes Punjabis are meant to do business.

Few days ago, he got a message from Anushka that Angira is going through a difficult phase, one that everyone goes through in life—Love. The foundation of every problem, and sometimes, a solution too.

Arjun and Anushka enter Coffee World. He takes his blazer off and they both sit in a cozy corner of the coffee shop.

'She wants to go to Mumbai, says Anushka.'

'So what's the problem if she wants to come to Mumbai?' Arjun asks

'There is no problem but after what happened in the past, Mom won't allow her to go out of town in this situation.' She looks worried and fiddles with the menu card as Arjun places an order for two cold coffees.

'Which situation?' he asks.

The waiter places two cups of coffee on the table.

'She is taking sleeping pills and Mom is worried about her. She doesn't listen to us. Everyone goes through a break up, but it doesn't mean that one has to ruin one's life over it. Now she says she wants to do fashion designing.'

Arjun pushes a cup of coffee on her side of the table. It's obvious that he cares for her and gets worried when she is in trouble.

'If she's so interested, she can just study from a good college in Delhi itself. There are so many good institutes in Delhi. She doesn't have to go to Mumbai,' he advises.

Anushka tears the sugar pouch and pours it into her cup. 'You want some sugar, too?'

Mulling over something, Arjun politely says no.

'Don't worry, things will be fine. I'll talk to her if you want,' he says.

'Yeah, sure. That might help.'

She continues taking long sips of the cold coffee. 'You know what, last week, at the dinner table we were talking about random things and then Angira started teasing me, saying that if I don't get married to you, she will.' They both burst out laughing, forgetting that they were at a coffee shop.

'What she needs is a good college,' he says, trying his best to digress. 'That should distract her from these random thoughts.'

'No, I am sure she likes you. Should I bring her to Mumbai?' she teases him.

'She's mad. You guys getting together will be the perfect combination—one will love me and the other will care for me.' he replies in jest.

'Shut up and listen,' she cuts him short but is herself filled with a sense of uncertainty over how Arjun will respond to what she's about to tell him.

'Yes, sure,' he replies with enthusiasm.

'Why don't you come to Delhi with me?' she says in one go. Before Arjun can say anything, she adds, 'And you are coming to Delhi next week anyhow. So prepone your schedule if you have any. You can meet Mom as well and tell her that you live in Mumbai. That will help Angira get her permission to go to Mumbai.'

'I am coming to Delhi next month, so we'll surely meet then,' he responds.

'I am talking about this week, Arjun,' she presses him.

He is utterly confused now. Why is she insisting on him meeting her mom so suddenly? Girls never tell everything at once, their secrets unfurl like in a game of cards. He knows that by the end of this, he is going to be either one of them—a Jack or a Joker.

'But what's the matter?' he asks, putting aside the cup which is not yet empty.

'Nothing. And it's not difficult for you to come with me tomorrow. You know Mom, she gives weight to your words. I just want to help Angira start a new life,' she says as she stirs her coffee.

'Anushka, my flight tickets are booked,' Arjun pleads, clasping his hands, still trying to figure out why she's so insistent.

When you are in trouble, you just need one person to pull you out of it. In his case, it was Anushka. He can't find a reason to say no to her. In fact, he doesn't even want to because in his worst days, it was she who stood by him when there was no one else. He decides to go to Delhi next week. Managing his itinerary should not be a problem.

'I expect you can afford cancelation charges and don't worry, I'll book the tickets for you,' she says.

'It's not about the ticket, it's...'

'Then you are coming to Delhi with me. I'll cancel your ticket and get the other one with me,' she says, grinning at him.

'Heads you win and tails I lose. Nicely played, Miss Anushka.'

'Yes, I have been smart since our college days.'

'That I am sure of, because in childhood you must have been really dumb!'

'Shut up! I was always smarter than you at least. And don't forget that I know all the naughty things you tried on your girlfriends during our college days.'

'I was immature at that time,' he says, trying to avoid having that discussion. 'Okay, I'll be coming with you. Over and out.'

'By the way, it's only you and me travelling together this time, so you can be sure you'll have a good time with me.'

'You are so smart,' he says

'Since the day I was born,' she winks while sipping her coffee.

After spending some time exploring the streets of Kolkata, they head back. The next day, they travel to Delhi.

Arjun feels ignored as Anushka constantly texts someone on their way to the arrival terminal at the New Delhi airport. He finds this behaviour a little discourteous. After trying to ignore it for a while, he can't take it anymore and speaks up.

'Who is messaging you continuously?'

They are both walking in the lobby of the airport.

'Oh! Somebody is feeling jealous, is it?' she mocks him.

'I am not feeling jealous, I am feeling ignored. There is a difference, isn't there?' He looks at her faking the expression of being in pain.

She starts laughing. 'You haven't changed in all these years. I think you still feel jealous.'

'Don't worry, I am not messaging any guy,' she added after a while.

Despite their differences, the two have developed a platonic relationship that Arjun won't risk for anything. It's a universal fact of friendship—that you can't see your best friend with anyone else.

'I am not saying that,' he says, trying to cover up his blunder.

'I'm sorry. I was texting Angira. She's just about to reach the airport to receive us. I think she's running late.'

She types out her last message and keeps her cellphone in the back pocket of her denim.

'Now, what are you trying to find down there?' she teases him for staring at her butt. 'Nice, isn't it?'

'Yes, very much, now let's go,' he says, ignoring her words.

Her cellphone rings.

'Where are you?' she asks the person on the other side who he assumes must be Angira.

He starts setting his hair and licking his lips to make them look fresh and lively. He calls them the natural and instant make-up tool for guys. He cannot pinch his cheeks in public to make them blush. Fortunately, he is never conscious in front of Anushka, who knows everything about him—from his waist size to his snoring.

'By the time you get ready, I will be there. So no need to come, Angy. I will be there in thirty minutes.' She looks at him and continues, 'Yes, he is with me, we both are coming.' She disconnects the call and keeps the phone back in her pocket.

They walk to Aerocity metro station to take the Airport Express to New Delhi metro station. Once in the cab, they gossip all the way to Anushka's home in Daryaganj.

❧

Anushka rings the bell. Standing at the door, a little girl smiles looking at her and says hello.

'Hi, how are you?' Anushka waves at her and smirks.

'I am good. Bye!' The young girl paddles her cycle away while giving her a flying kiss.

'Even kids are quite impressed by your jolly nature,' Arjun says, raising his eyebrows.

'That's in my blood,' she says with a certain amount of smugness.

As usual Arjun rearranges his clothes and sets his hair again.

'This sweet behaviour of yours doesn't work on me.' Arjun flashes a smile.

'You need to go to the doctor then,' she sniggers.

Creaking and groaning at the hinges, the door opens.

Dimpy aunty greets them. Arjun greets her by touching her feet.

'Where is Angy?' Anushka asks, throwing her bag on the sofa.

Arjun notices things have changed in Anushka's home since he was last there.

'She left to pick you up at the airport. But once you said you will come on your own, she decided to stop over at a friend's home. She should be home soon,' Dimpy aunty says with a smile, having seen Arjun after a long while.

She considers him to be her own son and Arjun has always been close to her.

'So you got a pug,' Arjun says while playing with the dog.

'These girls don't listen to me, so I needed someone at home who will listen to me,' she says.

Arjun laughs out loud.

'That was a pathetic joke, Mamma,' Anushka says while sitting on the sofa. 'Angira has been so careless. She left my hair dryer on in the room.'

'That's why I need this,' Dimpy aunty says, pointing at the pug.

'Mom, how does this pug help you switch off the hair dryer?' Anushka asks defiantly.

'Of course, he barks whenever something wrong happens.'

'Okay, Mom, we got it.'

Dimpy aunty winks at Arjun before asking, 'So how was the journey?'

'It was bound to be great because I came with her.'

'Well, actually Arjun wanted to meet you, that's why he has come with me,' Anushka says, looking at him.

He feels a little weird for a moment but he has to smile in front of Aunty. He enquires about what's going on in their household. Anushka says 'sorry' to him by holding her ears when her mom is not looking.

'It's great that you have come to meet us. By the way, any plans to apply some of that romance in real life or will it continue in books only?' Dimpy aunty teases him before going into the kitchen.

'I'm very hungry, just give me something to eat,' he says.

'You haven't changed at all,' Aunty runs her hand on his head.

Years have passed but Arjun has maintained his relationships in a way that they only become stronger with time.

Dimpy aunty is cheerful but also calm. She has a romantic husband who spends most of his time with her but these days he is travelling on some business. They have raised two girls together. While one is there with Arjun in the room, the other is yet to make an appearance.

'Ya mamma, I am hungry too,' Anushka demands some food.

'Just give me ten minutes,' Aunty replies from the kitchen.

'Arjun, come, I will show you my room.'

They go to the other room.

'It used to be the library when you had come last. We used to have such great discussions there,' Arjun says

'Yes, you were boring since college days,' she chuckles and takes him to her room.

The room is dark when they enter. Anushka switches on the lights. It seems the room is shared by Angira and Anushka. Arjun finds Angira's notebook on the table, a few cosmetics like lip-gloss, eyeliner, a bra in the corner of the bed and few of Anushka's pictures, with Angira and

Dimpy aunty, hanging on the wall just above the table. Anushka hides the clothes under the pillow before Arjun notices them. He lies down on the bed, staring at the ceiling.

'I am sorry, Arjun, about lying that time that you wanted to meet Mom but I had no other option.'

'That's okay. I know you didn't have any other option. What do we do now? Should I beg her to send Angira with me?'

'You know Mom very well, she'll listen to you. If you can assure her that you will be there for her and take Angira under your wings, then she will send her. Angira will be stuck here forever otherwise.'

He picks up a notebook. Turning the pages of the book, he notices the sketches on the last page.

'You sketch?' he asks her.

'That's Angira's,' she answers, taking the notebook from his hand. She sits next to him and the bed creaks.

'Anushka, start dieting,' he says, and immediately bursts out laughing.

She is a little embarrassed. 'Shut up! Are you done laughing?'

'So are all these related to fashion? These designs are really nice.'

He flips through the pages of the notebook while talking to Anushka about random things.

'I feel Angira needs to go out. She has changed a lot, but just because she is going through a heart break doesn't mean she should pause her life. I know she can manage herself very well. She just needs some time to get her life back together,' Anushka says.

'Hmm, I agree. So where is she? When is she coming home?'

'Must be on her way back by now.'

'So this is the only reason why you girls made me come from Kolkata to Delhi. You owe me a treat if Aunty agrees.'

'Promise,' Anushka says, crossing her fingers.

She is lying down on the bed next to Arjun.

'It's been a long time since you last came home,' she says, staring at the ceiling.

'Yes, more than two years.'

'Did you notice Mom? She became so happy after seeing you.

She misses a son in the family.' Anushka pushes his legs making more room for herself on the bed.

'I am always there for her. The son of this family...'

Arjun doesn't let her feel that she lost a brother and that Aunty lost her son in a road accident two years ago.

'I am hungry, let's go,' he says.

All Indian mothers operate from the kitchen.

Aunty announces, 'Arjun! Anushka! The food is ready.'

⁂

They all gather at the dining table in the hall, and relish each bite of the aloo parathas with curd and butter. Along with dinner, Dimpy aunty brings her humour to the table as well.

'Before marriage, Punjabi girls are hotter than the girls of any other state. After marriage, they are fatter than the women of any other state!'

'Speak of the devil and devil is here,' Anushka says as Angira appears in the hall.

'We were not talking about her, were we?' Arjun jokes.

'She'll kill you if I tell her what you just said,' Anushka says.

Arjun looks at Angira and murmurs, 'I didn't say anything.'

'Hey, how are you? I didn't say anything about you.'

Wearing a salwaar kameez and her hair in a braid with a ribbon, Angira looks like a typical Punjabi girl. Her natural jet black hair curls around her forehead. She looks rather cute with a reluctant smile. Her lips are pink, always ready to curve into a smile. She has the perfect curves. At five feet four inches, with beautiful eyes and red cheeks, her soft and flawless skin possesses a natural glow, almost radiating a positive energy.

'I am good. Hope you are doing well. Good to see you home,' Angira says, smiling.

'Yeah,' he replies while eating the last bite of his paratha.

Keeping his word to Anushka, he asks Dimpy aunty, 'So Aunty, Anushka told me that Angira is coming to Mumbai for fashion designing.'

'Yes, she wants to,' Aunty says from the kitchen.

'When is she going then?'

'Beta, we don't know anyone there. It's a new city. I am telling her to get into a good college in Delhi if she really wants to study.'

'Oh Mom, don't start again. I have decided, that's it,' Angira says, and goes to her room.

'See,' Aunty says, frustrated with her daughter's tantrums.

'Every day we hear something in the news. So I asked her to look for something here in Delhi. I don't feel safe sending her out of town,' her mom explains. She has already lost a son. There's no way she is going to leave her daughters alone.

'That's true but Mumbai is a safer place, you know. She can go there if she wants to go. I saw her sketches in the room and she really has potential,' Arjun openly declares his support for Angira.

'Yes, mamma, he really liked them. I mean he is impressed.' Anushka adds, trying to make a strong case on behalf of Angira.

In Arjun's mind, things are taking a different direction. He is not sure yet about looking after Angira in Mumbai. What if something happens to her in the future that Dimpy aunty might not appreciate?

Angira comes back and joins them.

By the way mamma, because Arjun is there in Mumbai, if Angira wants any help she can simply call him. Plus, living in a new city might help her feel better as well.' Anushka looks at Angira and then at Arjun.

'Yes, I agree,' Arjun says while smiling reassuringly.

'Yes, Mom, please let me go. My friend Charu is also going, please. I will study hard, promise. Please...please...please,' Angira pleads.

'How will you manage your accommodation and food there?' she asks, finally showing signs of agreement. She is warming up to the idea, but her heart is still not completely convinced.

'I can take care of that, don't worry. If she wants to come to Mumbai, let her come, but she must promise that she will study hard. No late night parties.' Arjun puts forward his conditions, though he knows Angira will not follow these rules.

Angira gives him a puzzled glance as to why he would say the last sentence—'No late night parties'—because her mom anyway doesn't know about the night-outs she goes for.

'Yes, I promise, Mom. Let me call Charu.' She texts someone on the phone.

Arjun understands that things seem to be going as per plan for Angira, but he's still clouded with doubts. He realizes that one can walk with someone but can't walk for someone.

'I don't have any problem sending her to Mumbai, but given what happened with her in the past I am really scared,' Dimpy aunty says while seating herself on the sofa.

'Mom, let's not go there. Everything is fine now. So why are you worried?'

'But...'

'No ifs and buts, everything is fine, Mom. Let me go,' Angira says, kissing her mom on the cheeks.

'Ask your father once,' Dimpy aunty says.

'I have already informed Papa that I got into a good college. He was waiting for your green signal!' Angira seems set with her plan.

Arjun is just listening to the whole conversation like a school kid in a classroom.

'Okay, so everything is done. Happy? Now go pack your bags and get ready,' Anushka announces.

'Mom, make us some coffee for now. I am taking these guys out later and will drop Arjun as well. He needs to catch his flight back to Mumbai. I will call you if I get late.'

'Coffee is ready,' Angira says.

She looks like the real Angira now—happy and cheerful.

'You came just for a day?' Aunty questions Arjun.

'Yes, I came for some work and thought I must drop by to meet you. I have to come again next week,' he says, giving Anushka a nervous glance.

'But you...'

'I couldn't prepone the plan,' Arjun tells Anushka. She remains silent.

'Very nice, beta. Thanks for coming here. Come again. Whenever you come, I feel so happy,' Dimpy aunty says while Anushka and

Arjun are busy gossiping.

'Adopt me then,' he says, making her laugh. That is what she likes best about him—his ability to make someone laugh no matter how tense the situation gets.

These are Arjun's best known qualities amongst his loved ones—to infuse every moment with humour and the tendency to look ahead with a positive attitude.

'Anytime, beta,' Aunty runs her hand over his head.

Anushka hands over the car keys to Arjun as they begin preparing for their departure.

'Am I going to drive?' he asks.

'Yes. While you are in Delhi,' she responds.

'But I don't know the roads here.'

'You have roamed around more than I have for sure. Don't make me open my mouth,' Anushka mumbles so that Dimpy aunty cannot hear their conversation.

Arjun smiles and remembers how years ago he used to roam around the streets of Delhi with Anushka by his side.

Arjun is ready within minutes, and after seeking blessings from Dimpy aunty, he leaves with Anushka and Angira.

'It was nice meeting you. You can come anytime you want to.' Aunty pats on the back of his head when he touches her feet. She gives him her blessings, 'Rab rakha puttar, jeeta reh.'

'It always makes me so happy to meet you Aunty, and I'll miss your aloo parathas with curd and butter!' Arjun says with a smile.

'You sit comfortably, I'll drive,' Angira says, taking the keys from Arjun and getting inside the car.

He sits on the backseat of the car with Anushka.

'Thanks a lot, Arjun,' Angira says while putting on the seat belt.

'For? Convincing your Mom to let you go to Mumbai, is it?'

'Yes, Mom wasn't ready as you know,' she says, as she accelerates and drives the car.

'The credit goes to her. She brought me here and lied to Aunty saying that I wanted to meet her.'

'I didn't lie. I just manipulated a little. By the way, lies are not lies if they are spoken for good reasons.'

'Oh, my philosopher,' Arjun says in an exasperated voice.

'Actually, this was our plan. I was aware of it,' Angira says. 'Let's drop the subject. No point going on about it. What's done is done. Let me take you somewhere we haven't been before.'

'You both will get me in trouble one day,' Arjun says.

Angira slows down in front of a karaoke lounge bar.

'Are we going in there?' Arjun asks, feeling relaxed now that he does not have to convince anyone anymore.

'Yup, today is your day. This place is all yours,' Anushka says pointing at the lounge.

∞

'You know I don't sing,' he says, smiling.

'Shut up and come quietly. I know everything about you. What you do, what you don't,' Anushka says as they get out of the car.

They enter one of the best karaoke houses in Delhi—a vibrant, upscale leisure destination for those who believe food is for the tummy and music is for the soul.

'Wouldn't you just love to get high and embarrass yourself in front of everyone?' Anushka pokes Arjun in his waist.

'Is it? I am always embarrassed when I am with you.'

'Oh thank you, thank you. So go ahead, discover the singer in you,' Anushka nods.

The menu is irresistible with classic vegetarian and non-vegetarian dishes and salads. The ambience with its dim-lighting and cozy décor is romantic to say the least. Everything looks just perfect. Angira is about to say something but she takes a sip of water and leans back instead.

Arjun orders Paneer-e-Shola, while Anushka asks for Kakori Kebab. Angira decides to skip food altogether and asks the waiter for vodka with orange juice.

'Make that two,' Anushka says with a smile. 'You want some?' she asks Arjun.

'No, I am good,' he says.

'So have you also come here for the first time?' he asks Angira while Anushka is busy texting someone.

Though she replies with a nod, he senses that there's something on her mind. He decides not to ask anything further.

'So are you still single?' Angira asks, fiddling with the potato skins on her plate.

'Yes.'

'Either you aren't able to get the right girl or you are too reclusive. Which one is it?' she asks with a husky voice.

Clearly taken aback, he shrugs his shoulders. 'May be. I need to analyse this tragedy.'

They both laugh.

There is an unexpected announcement, 'Now let's have a big round of applause for Anushka!'

Anushka looks stunned as people clap for her, forcing her to come to the karaoke area.

'Go, this is all yours.' Arjun shows her the way towards the stage.

'I'll kill you. Did you give them my name?'

'It's already announced, go... Now go and rock the floor,' he repeats.

She gives her cellphone to Angira and goes to the stage confidently.

'She is good at singing,' Angira declares proudly.

'Yeah, I had heard her during our college days,' Arjun says as Anushka is walking to the stage.

Anushka holds the microphone. Music starts to play in the background and everyone is stunned the moment Anushka's voice comes on.

This is where I long to be

La isla bonita

'She is so much better at singing now.' Arjun is glad that he is enjoying the day with these mischievous sisters, which he didn't think was even a possibility earlier.

'I told you,' Angira says with a knowing look.

'Very nice, Miss Anushka.' Arjun gives her a glass of water.

'Hey, I need my cellphone,' Anushka takes her phone. 'I'll come back in five minutes.'

'So what happened? Anushka told me a little bit, but I wanted to ask you in person.'

Angira takes a large sip of vodka, before looking at him to answer. 'Who knows better than you that when you love someone more than anything and they leave you for no reason, then you just breathe but don't really live. Am I right?'

'Correct,' Arjun nods.

'You know, Arjun, I had faith in God but whatever happened in my past has turned me into an atheist. There is no God in the world. There is just a...' She doesn't say anything for a while before finishing with a smile, '...let's not go there.'

'I can only say that things happen for a reason and for a good cause.' He lets the waiter serve the drink that he ordered for Anushka when she had gone to sing. Anushka joins them back.

'Sometimes I feel like finding a rich guy even if he doesn't love me because people eventually ditch you anyway. At least if I know he doesn't love me, it'll hurt less.'

'It seems like three shots of vodka have done the trick,' Anushka comments.

Angira is emotional. People behave weirdly after drinking actually, because that's when the truth comes out. They say what they have always wanted to say, but never had the courage to do so. And this very behaviour is considered 'weird' by society.

Arjun finishes his glass of beer.

'What?'

'Now it's your turn,' she says, sounding playful and revengeful all at once.

'The sun will rise tomorrow so just get up and keep walking. Don't stop.' He tells Angira he'll be back soon.

'You are going to sing? Seriously? Oh my goodness. I am blessed. Go! Go! Go!'

Arjun is not only a guitarist but a decent singer as well. He reaches the stage and holds the microphone in his hand, and looks into Angira's eyes.

'For the sisters who accompanied me to this karaoke bar tonight,' he says with a smile.

I'll love you long after you go.
And long after you're gone gone gone.

Once the song finishes, everyone gives Arjun a standing ovation.

'You were just OMG,' Angira says to him in amazement.

'Thanks,' he replies shyly.

Forgetting Social Boundaries

'Let's go, we need to get Arjun inside the girls' hostel,' Anushka looks at Angira with a naughty smile.

'What? Are you mad? I don't want to get into trouble. I am not going anywhere,' Arjun replies firmly.

He is enjoying spending time with them but it is not fun jumping the wall of a girls' hostel, especially when you've had one too many beers.

'Oh come on! Don't be such a spoilsport,' Anushka says with a giggle.

'I am not a spoilsport. I just don't want to go to jail. I know how terrifying Delhi can be.'

Anushka pinches him and pulls him by his arm outside the bar while Angira pays for the meal.

'Come on, let's go.'

'Don't get mad, but I won't. I haven't done these things in my life.' He gets up and adds, 'And I have to leave early tomorrow morning as well when you both will be sleeping in bed. So I better get some rest.'

'Oh, my sensitive lad,' Anushka says cynically.

'You only said, things happen for a reason. So, let our wish be the reason for you to get inside a girls' hostel.' Angira signs on the receipt and looks at him rather sharply.

'Don't worry, you are safe. Actually few of my friends want to meet you. We will go for some time and then we'll come back soon,' Anushka assures him, mischief in her eyes.

'Where do they live?'

'Saket.'

'Anushka, it's 11 p.m. You will drive to Saket at this hour?' Arjun is least interested in going out with her right now.

Though he is cool and open-minded, he can also be somewhat reserved. He is not the kind of person who can call and chat with anyone at any time. Moreover, right now he is worried about his departure.

'I don't know them and I know you are going to turn me into a showpiece in front of them,' he says, following her footsteps.

'Chill and come quietly,' she says as she pulls his hand and they walk out the exit.

After an alcohol-laced evening, Anushka drives to the girls' hostel. It's easy to guess from the clothes that are hanging on the railing of the balconies. Arjun is familiar with these hostels.

'Can't we ask him to open the gate?' Arjun asks, as he steps out of the car and walks towards the gate while Angira follows him.

'You really want to do that or what?' Anushka teases him and continues, 'No, wait. I know how to go inside.'

Anushka parks the car and puts the keys in her handbag. She walks confidently to the security guard's room.

'Don't kick him in his balls,' Angira murmurs, and takes half a step back. 'Now see how your friend deals with the situation.'

Anushka wakes the guard up. The security guard rubs his eyes and looks at them irritably.

'What happened?' he asks.

'Can you open the gate?' she asks him casually.

The guard looks at his cellphone and says, 'It's 12.15 a.m. I can't open the gate at this time.' He points towards Arjun. 'And who is he? Boys are not allowed to enter. It is an order from Singh Sahab. Talk to him first.'

Anushka says, 'Uncle, actually his sister lives here and today is her birthday, and he has come from Mumbai just to give her a surprise. He will feel bad if you don't allow him inside. And we just need to see her for an hour.'

He stares at her. 'But boys are not allowed. Call her sister at the gate if you want.'

Arjun remains silent like he was instructed. Angira steps back and whispers, 'Why are you so quiet?'

'Because getting inside a girls' hostel is a crime and I don't want to spend my life in jail, that too for such a stupid reason,' Arjun replies.

'Chill,' she says with a big smile.

Angira takes her cellphone out and calls someone.

'Hey, we are at your gate but it's locked. The guard is not opening the gate.'

The guard looks at Angira who stares back at him confidently. Everything in life can be achieved if you're confident enough. Arjun got his job offer by giving a confident interview.

'Strike while the iron is hot' is what Anushka believes in.

'Bhaiya, take it. I am going with him, you don't worry.'

Anushka gives him a packet of cigarettes and a sweet smile which is enough for the guard to open the gate.

He looks around.

'You smoke these till we're back,' Anushka assures him.

Hiding the packet of cigarettes inside his jacket, he says, 'Don't make noise and go silently.'

He does not even ask which room they have to go to. He gives a worn out register to Arjun to put his entry in it. Angira decides to sign on behalf of Arjun and scribbles some obscure name that even she cannot read and mentions a phone number with her signature. The guard opens the door and they enter.

❧

'You should experience all the colours of life,' Angira says, pulling his hand.

For a moment, Arjun feels nervous as he follows her inside the premises. Anushka rings the bell. Arjun is afraid of being seen and can't wait to get inside the room.

The door opens with shrieks of joy.

'Hey!' Charu hugs Anushka, abuses Angira jokingly and just waves at Arjun.

Arjun responds with a courteous smile.

Charu is Angira's best friend and classmate. They both are planning to go to Mumbai together. Charu wants to study further just to be away from family and relatives, so that they do not force her to get married so soon. She questions the need to get married, especially when she can do something better with her life.

'Hi guys, come on in,' Mansi says, getting up from the corner of the hall. Mansi is a friend of Anushka's. A student of Mathematics in Miranda House, her passion is photography and she has applied to the New York Institute of Photography for a course next year.

Mansi and Charu take them to the bedroom because the hall is messy. It seems they have been partying. Arjun starts exploring the room upon entering. A girl gets up from the other corner of the room in a hurry and says hello to everyone.

Though places are an extension of human behaviour and personality, it's impossible for one to guess the personality of a person by looking at their hostel room. The room has pink curtains and a rust-coloured bed that is set against the backdrop of white- panelled walls. There are a few soft toys on the bed. Two red cups are placed on the stool. There's a large table in the corner of the room and adjacent to the bed, a ping-pong table lies unused.

'Looking pretty,' Mansi says, giving a hug to Anushka.

'Thanks.'

'You guys already know Arjun. Arjun, this is Mansi and Charu,' Anushka introduces them with a smile.

'Hi,' Arjun says and they offer him a place to sit while Charu is clearing the mattress in the hall.

Charu dumps the mattress on the floor so everyone can sit comfortably.

'We were waiting for you,' Charu informs Angira.

'We heard about you from Angira and Anushka, so we thought of calling you for our girls' party. I hope you are comfortable here,' Charu says, passing him the bottle of soft drink.

'He must be,' Mansi says. 'I have read your previous books, quite impressive. You know girls very well.'

'Thank you,' he says modestly.

'Lots of new stuff for you to learn here amongst us and include in your next book,' she says, trying to make Arjun comfortable.

'Yes, sure. Tonight was such a different experience with these sisters. This opportunity to visit a girls' hostel came out of the blue. But yes, it's definitely exciting.'

'You guys want to eat something?' Charu asks.

'No, I am stuffed,' Arjun says.

Mansi takes the hookah out of her cupboard and places it in the centre of the hall.

'This is for all of you,' she says.

Anushka winks at Arjun, trying to gauge if he is comfortable. He smiles back. Arjun has never tried hookah before, not even in his college where his friends smoked bong and weed. Charu and Angira get chips and potato swirls from the kitchen.

'Do you guys have these parties often?' he asks casually.

Mansi, Angira and Charu laugh together. Arjun notices Anushka texting someone over WhatsApp.

'No, only on weekends if they are free. That's our gang,' Mansi says.

'And it's not injurious to health?'

Charu jumps in, 'Yeah, but life is more injurious.' She gives him a funny look and passes the hookah to him.

'Don't worry, it is flavoured hookah. It doesn't taste like tobacco at all. You must try it,' Mansi says.

'If he doesn't want, don't force him. He has to catch his flight back to Mumbai,' Anushka adds.

'No, he has to try this for us,' she teases him, holding the pipe in her hand and taking a long puff from it. The coal on top burns violently as she sucks it in.

'I have heard somewhere that this aids the ability to think and concentrate, so people like you should really try this,' Mansi hands over the pipe to Angira.

Angira takes the pipe from her and at first she does not inhale the smoke. She just sucks some smoke in and holds it in her mouth before blowing it out

'Nice, you are good at it,' Arjun remarks, observing each attempt of hers.

'You know what, I have a love–hate relationship with cigarettes, hookah and getting high. There's such an intense pleasure in getting high that you can't even get from spending time with your boyfriend in bed,' she finishes her words and laughs aloud with the others. Having had hookah after drinks, Angira is completely out of her senses.

The room is full of smoke. Mansi rolls her eyes and tells Angira to stop wasting the hookah. Angira passes the hookah to Arjun this time and he is willing to try it. He takes a small puff. It does not taste terrible, however it smells like household chemicals. Arjun inhales the smoke and pushes a small amount of air out of his lower throat without taking a breath and without moving his lower jaw. The first ring comes out in the air.

'Hey, it's there, it's there!' exclaims Angira and touches the ring with her fingers and it vanishes in the air.

'I have just tried once or twice but you know confidence matters,' Arjun winks this time.

Angira looks jolly and happy. She tries to create smoke rings, but she can hardly make any. Few rings come out half, few others come out just as smoke. Only the few from Arjun come out in rings and go higher and higher, dancing in the air. Everyone takes turns to create these rings but no one is successful. Everyone laughs at their failure.

Arjun says, 'Guys, I need to leave in some time, my cab is reaching here in fifteen minutes.'

'You just came an hour ago,' Charu complains.

'But I need to go, it's important,' he says, checking his watch.

'Should I drop you?' Anushka asks him and at the same moment Angira wants to say something but stops.

'No, the cab is coming.'

'Why would you go in a cab when I am here for you?' Anushka gets up and tells Mansi to come with her.

'Anushka, it's too late, stay here. The cab is on the way.'

'Don't worry, her brother is a Senior Superintendent of Police,' Anushka assures him.

'I'll wait for you in Mumbai. Let me know once you reach there,' Arjun tells Angira. 'Thanks Charu and Mansi, it was nice meeting you. See you again. Let's go, Anushka.'

Angira nods, smiling at him. Arjun thanks everyone for their hospitality and waves his hand. Mansi follows them to the stairs. They all come downstairs and tell the guard to open the gate while he is smoking and enjoying the cold night.

Anushka tells the guard that he'll have to open the gate again when she returns. Arjun calls the cab driver and cancels the ride, as he gets inside Anushka's car. The moment Arjun leaves with Anushka and Mansi, a cab arrives from the opposite end, takes a U-turn and stops at the gate where Charu and Angira just entered. The guard has woken up again and recognizes that a cab has just arrived. He hides the cigarettes and gulps down the smoke.

We Party All Night

Iona waves her hand in excitement. 'Hey girls, what's up? What are you girls doing at the gate in the middle of the night. Someone was robbed or what?' Iona steps out of the cab.

'Hey, I thought you were not coming,' Charu says.

'I was at a family dinner, so I got late,' Iona replies and pays the driver.

'This is Angira. Angira this is Iona, your sister's close friend,' Charu introduces them.

'Hey, hi…'

Iona is a close friend of Anushka's and Mansi's. Hence, Charu too has become a good friend recently. Iona is an easy-going person. She is an engineer and a passionate traveller. She is confident, spontaneous and outgoing. She is also a couch surfer (couch surfing involves letting someone, who cannot afford an elite place, stay in your house while visiting a new place and they in turn let you stay in their house if you ever visit their city) and has travelled to thirty-two cities. Her dream is to walk the globe someday. Her family doesn't support her. Many a times she has had arguments with them because they consider couch surfing against their culture.

Iona is a hipster and fashion freak. Today she is wearing a funky shirt with swear words printed on it and an image showing the middle finger.

'Nice tee, Iona,' Charu says pointing out to her shirt

'Yeah, this is for those guys who stare at women and make us uncomfortable,' she laughs

The guard stares at Iona while lighting his cigarette.

'Let's go inside.' Angira moves back upstairs and both follow her. Charu unlocks the door.

'So you guys are already having a party,' Iona says, noticing the hookah and other stuff lying on the floor. She sits on the couch and looks outside from the sliding window. Iona takes something out from her pocket and hands it to Charu, 'Keep it somewhere.'

'That's like a good girl,' Charu takes the packet and keeps it under the mattress.

'Is that weed? Where did you score this?' Angira asks Iona curiously.

Though Angira has never had weed before, she guesses correctly because she had seen her friends smoking it during their college days.

'I went to Shimla last week to attend a fest in my friend's college. I got some good stuff there,' she winks at Charu.

'Do you have cigarettes?' Iona asks Angira.

'I don't smoke,' she replies.

'Oh! No problem.'

Angira's cellphone rings. It's Anushka. She attends the call.

'What happened?' she asks.

'Nothing, I am going home. Mom is alone. Don't drink any more and don't come at night. But be there at the breakfast table tomorrow morning. I'll tell Mom that you are with your friends.'

'Okay,' Angira replies and continues, 'drive safely and text me once you reach home.'

❧

After some time the door opens and Mansi enters.

'Oh my god, look who has come!' Mansi runs to Iona and hugs her tightly.

'I came after you left,' Iona says.

They all start talking about their crushes. Mansi gets a packet of cigarettes and she takes one out of the box. Charu takes that small packet and gives it to Iona. Iona puts a little weed on the newspaper and starts crushing it.

'Go and get the cone cool box,' Iona asks Mansi.

'What is a cone cool box?' asks Angira and makes a guess, 'Is that a box to make a roll?'

'Smart ass you are,' Iona replies and everyone laughs.

Angira ignores the joke.

'It's not there. Mansi's parents came last week so we threw it in the backyard,' Charu says.

Iona shoves her hand in her back pocket and gets a visiting card from her wallet. She cuts a small square of about half an inch and rolls it between her fingers.

'Pass me the paper,' she says to Mansi.

She puts weed on the paper and rolls in gently while putting a bud at one end.

She licks the edge of the paper and sticks it. While sticking, the entire weed comes out of the roll and Angira bursts out laughing. Angira's sarcasm was an obvious comeback because few minutes ago Iona had laughed at her.

'It's okay,' Mansi says while putting the weed back on the paper.

'Is something wrong?' Charu asks, sensing the tension.

'We are perfectly fine,' they both say in the same tone, as if they were trained to synchronize their voices.

Iona does crazy things on her own and her creative ideas impress everyone who are already high on weed. Angira looks comfortable and happy in her company.

'You girls are crazy,' Mansi says with a smile.

Angira and Iona might have one or two mainstream interests, like yoga, but they also have some uncommon interests like bee-keeping and quilting. They enjoy this night together because Angira is moving to Mumbai and they don't know when all of them will see each other again. The world is small. May be one day they will see each other again, but for now, tonight is all they have.

'If you have never smoked anything, it might be a bit harsh to inhale,' Iona says while lighting the roll of weed.

'No, I have tried this in college once,' Angira says with confidence

'Seriously? You told me that you never did,' Charu asks her, surprised.

'Just one puff.'

'Ooo! You're a secretive one!' Iona gives her the joint to smoke and shares her expert advice, 'Take a slow deep puff. Then breathe it in slowly and exhale just as slowly. Take it slow and stop, then pause a second and then slowly blow it all out.'

Time slows down and Iona and Angira begin feeling like they are old friends. The smoke brings out their sadness, wraps itself around their worries. Soon Mansi and Charu join in too and the party remains within this closed circle of friends. Mansi ends up making a thank you speech to Iona for making the party special for everyone. Angira too feels like herself again after a very long time. Her tragic break-up few weeks ago left her high and dry. Charu and Mansi are aware of Angira's situation and have tried their best to pull her out from her past. It is difficult for her to forget, but any pain takes time to heal and today she seems to have recovered a bit more than before.

'I am thinking of going home,' Angira says, taking a long puff and handing over the remaining joint to Charu.

'Are you sure, at this time?' Iona asks and laughs aloud and carries on, 'This shows you are out, which is nice. This is how parties begin!' She opens the bottle of vodka and pours it into some shot glasses.

'Have a shot of this, it's no less than magic,' Iona makes a small peg and gives to her.

Angira checks her cellphone and messages someone. All of a sudden, she looks uncomfortable. Whenever she drinks, she becomes sentimental. She wants to enjoy her life but something always comes in the way. It feels like she has locked herself in a room and decided not to open the door for anyone.

Snapping her fingers, Iona passes her a plate of chips and asks, 'What are you upto?'

'Nothing.' Angira ignores her.

When things have to happen, they happen without our knowledge. Iona brings out the bruises in Angira's heart.

'So what does your boyfriend do?' Iona asks her.

Mansi and Charu look at Iona who is unaware of the consequences of this question, but they know that Angira could break into tears any moment. Angira chooses to smile instead and calmly sips her vodka.

'So where are you headed next?' Mansi asks Iona with the intention to change the discussion which was about to start.

'Next destination is Kerala,' she responds and asks Angira the same question while she texts someone.

'Who are you talking to, babes? Let him live his life. That's the problem with girls. That's why boys find happiness outside because you trouble them a lot.'

'Who?' Angira asks, puzzled.

'Your man,' Iona says.

Coffee Is Old, Vodka Is New

Angira finishes her glass of vodka, takes a moment and then begins talking to Iona.

'There is no guy in my life because love sucks,' she says, smiling to herself.

'O-o, I am so sorry if I have asked anything wrong. I was just annoyed with you for texting constantly,' Iona apologises, aware of the fact that she crossed the line.

Sometimes friendship doesn't take much time to grow; sometimes it takes root within that shared moment when two people act in a selfless manner. The same happened with Iona and Angira.

'No, that's fine but believe me, love sucks,' Angira says, emphasizing the last two words.

'But why do you think so?' Charu asks her. Though she knows what Angira has gone through, she wants her to speak about whatever is on her mind and let it out.

No relationship can be defined by a few bad experiences someone has gone through. Being her close friend, Charu has told her to move on and forget everything that has happened because memories are something that can't be erased. You can only create the good ones by moving on.

Angira pours some more vodka in her glass and leans on the wall, 'Leave it, no point discussing things which gave me nightmares.'

She takes another sip of her drink.

'Hey Angira, chill, tell me what happened. I'll surely help you. I have seen many people suffering from relationships and love,' Iona pops into the discussion proactively.

Angira looks lost, pressing the tip of her fingers on the glass and holding it tightly. She suddenly changes her mind and decides to tell them her story.

'I don't know if I should talk about it, but since Mansi and Charu know everything about me and I am drunk, maybe I can muster the courage to talk about my dejected life.'

'That's fine,' Mansi pats on her shoulder.

Being a traveller, Iona has met thousands of people. She believes that a heartbreak is the best time as your creativity comes out and you do something extraordinary. Iona wants Angira to find her passion and nurture it.

She sounds like she wants to help Angira.

'So what happened to your relationship?' Iona questions.

'Do you really want to know?' Angira asks one more time.

'Yes, I can help you,' Iona says confidently. Being her well-wisher she gives her a gentle smile.

Angira keeps the glass aside and stretches her legs. She starts, 'It's not fun to talk about but yes, I was in college when I met him for the first time. He was from Delhi too and slowly we became good friends. Soon we became the best of friends, without any obligations or boundaries. We were like soulmates. We never thought about love and sex, but we were close emotionally. We shared everything, from class notes to our happiness and pain. Eventually our friends started saying that we were in love. We gave a new definition to our friendship and that went on for three years during college, yes three years, and we didn't even kiss each other. He was the type of friend one would never want to lose because he had the ability to make you feel good.

'In the last year of college, I realized that he had feelings for me but I never took things forward and always treated him like my 4 a.m. friend. One night he sent me a video on WhatsApp, of him playing his guitar on the terrace of the hostel. He dedicated that beautiful song to me.

'After that he told me to come out of the hostel because he wanted to show me something. The hostel was partially CO-ED, only separated by a wall and a few irresponsible guards. Somehow we always managed to jump over the wall and go for late night walks.

'Surprisingly, he proposed to me. I knew he liked me but never expected that he would propose to me. This was an emotional moment for me. It's a dream of every girl that someone should love her more than anything in life. I was on top of the world but somewhere I was afraid too. I had seen my friends heartbroken over failed relationships before. So I took time to make my decision. On the last day of our semester exams, we had our first kiss in the boys' hostel washroom.'

'You guys kissed in a boys' toilet? Seriously?' Iona asks.

Angira continues with an expressionless face.

'It was a risk, but we both enjoyed the moment. We were scared when one of our friends noticed us and then I had to tell her everything and advise her not to let it become college gossip. I was in a different world. Many times it happens that you can't discuss everything with a girl and in fact it's a guy who ends up coming to your rescue. He was there whenever I needed him. We started meeting in the corners of our college campus. We went on a few overnight trips.

'We came closer and closer and I started to like everything about him. When college was over, I started calling him over when my family wasn't around.

'After a few months I came to know that he was cheating on me, but I didn't believe it. I tried my best to fix things but nothing worked out. We started fighting about random things. He was involved with someone else and left me when he felt like I had become dependent on him.

'My life turned upside down. I did not know what to do for the longest time. Nothing was working out for me anymore. Surrendering to my destiny was not something I wanted to do. Everything that has a beginning, has an end too. We refuse to believe in this because we feel our love is immortal. We never met again. My perception of love changed after this. How life changes in the blink of an eye. That day I realized that my guy needed me for my body and not for love. I lost my faith in love and love lost me forever.

'That's the story of my fucking love life that you were so curious to know about,' Angira says with a sense of numbness.

Everyone is just stunned. This was unexpected for everyone. Iona feels sorry for her loss but being an eternal optimist, she says, 'It happens, Angira. Things will get better though.'

'And that's how this became my friend,' Angira says, pointing to the glass of vodka, and the weed. 'I know, I am not supposed to talk about my personal matters. After all, it's my life and I am responsible for it. I hope you won't judge me for all this. I just found the courage to speak up.'

'Hey, that's perfectly fine,' Mansi says and adds, 'we share things with friends because they give us the strength to face it.'

Iona interrupts in between, 'So that's okay, this is just a phase of life. Love is game of bluff. You can't know a person unless you've spent a lot of time with them. That's the only way of finding out.'

Angira realizes that she has said too much. At this moment she is missing Anushka, who has always helped her in any situation.

'I was done with life. I started overdosing on sleeping pills. Eventually, my mom came to know about my situation. Since that day she never leaves me alone. That's the reason she wasn't ready to send me to Mumbai, but she finally agreed today,' Angira says.

Mansi pats on her shoulder and says, 'Everything is an experience in life. So you had one, that's it. Just learn and leave.'

'It doesn't affect me as much as it used to. I feel I am stronger now,' Angira says, with a triumphant smile.

'Smart ass,' Iona teases her, poking her on her waist.

She takes a few long drags of the cigarette and slowly blows the smoke out of her mouth and nose. Angira laughs with them.

'Yes, let's go to Mumbai. It's going to be awesome. I am so excited!' Charu looks enthusiastically at Angira.

Angira announces loudly in front of the rest, 'By the way, she is a fucking great designer.'

'That's great, all the best. I am sure you'll rock it,' Iona wishes her and everyone looks happy for her.

Angira thanks everyone for having this get-together. 'Thanks. And this is my last party with you guys in Delhi. I am going to Mumbai, so keep in touch. I'll miss you all badly and especially our discussions on the chutiyapa of life.'

'Seriously, this was fun. Don't worry, we'll catch up once you are in Mumbai,' Mansi says.

'Sure.'

Everyone is completely drunk. Angira and Charu are completely zoned out as it was their first time trying weed properly.

'I think I am going to pass out,' Angira says. 'How will I go home?'

'Don't worry, you will be fine by tomorrow,' Mansi says, passing her a bottle of water.

'Okay, then let's not stop the party,' Angira shouts and asks for another glass of vodka.

Everyone exchanges numbers and promises to keep in touch.

'I'll see you if I come to Mumbai, maybe on my next trip,' Iona smiles and gives Angira a high five.

'Sure.'

Now Charu is busy with her phone and Mansi is sleepy after having had one too many drinks. With smoke, empty glasses, cigarette ash all over the floor, they pass out, too tired to clean the mess.

The next morning, Angira leaves after opening the gate silently while the guard is sleeping. Angira's cellphone beeps. It's a message from Arjun:

> Good morning! The best karma in life is to heal someone's pain.
> And you are not just my best friend's sister, but also my friend.
> I have done what I had to. Welcome to Mumbai!

Angira replies while crossing the road and hailing an autorickshaw:

> Thanks a lot for that.
> And you can call me Angira.
> Best friend's sister sounds
> like the title of a porn video.
> Haha!

Angira smiles on her way home in the autorickshaw. She has to go for shopping with Anushka and start packing for Mumbai.

Ved, the New Guy

'I have just reached the hotel room. It's a nice place. Yes, Mom, they have provided the accommodation for three weeks. Charu and I are sharing the room and then we will shift to a PG.' She unlocks the door and drags her giant trolley bag inside. She manages to come in and keep the bag in the corner of the hall.

Charu follows her and lies down on the sofa in the hall. 'Angy, do you have a water bottle?'

Angira nods.

'No, not hungry, I had enough in the train. Just that my hands are itching.'

Angira checks out the place while talking to her mom.

She enters the kitchen and checks the refrigerator to see if there's any water bottle in it.

'What the fu...' she says in frustration but stops without completing her sentence when she realizes her mom is listening on the other end.

'What happened?' her mom asks.

'Nothing, it's too humid here, Mom.'

'I told you, you won't be able to adjust.'

Angira realizes her folly. She completes her sentence saying, 'but yesterday it rained, so the weather is nice, just a little humid for some time.'

'Take care of yourself, and if you feel like, you can call Arjun. I spoke with him this morning.' Her mom is a little worried as this is the first time Angira has been out of Delhi.

'Mom, don't worry. If I need any help, I'll call him. I am on roaming, so I have to go to the service centre to get the portability for my number. But I am perfectly fine. You take care of yourself and I love you.' She finds a sealed water bottle on the table but, on drinking it she feels like it was boiled a minute ago. She drinks it anyway and passes the bottle to Charu, who is lying down like a dead person. Angira sits on the chair with her elbow on the dining table.

'Yes, I'm going to take a bath. Will call you in the evening,' she says and disconnects the call.

She goes to one of the rooms and lies down on the bed, recalling the moments she spent last week with Iona, Anushka, Arjun and her friends in Delhi. She grins as she looks at the ceiling. She turns a little and looks at her reflection on the mirror of the dressing table which is in front of the bed. She takes her phone out from her pocket and scrolls up and down on WhatsApp, checking out the photographs which Anushka sent to her. Randomly, she moves to Arjun's WhatsApp profile picture. She types 'hi' in the chat-window and then stops upon realizing that he might be in office at this moment. She decides against texting him and scrolls down. She texts Iona casually to know when she is coming to Mumbai.

Hey! How are you? I have a surprise for you.

Iona is online on WhatsApp and Angira gets a reply within seconds. Iona is typing...

I am fine. Oh really, what's that?

Charu walks into the room to check the cupboards while Angira is texting Iona.

I have reached Mumbai. When are you coming?
And who is this charming guy in your profile picture.
Is this your boyfriend? ;)
Ahem...ahem.

The screen flashes with a new message.

I am also here in Mumbai.
How's the DP? Did you like him?

Angira's mind fills with plans of roaming around with Iona before their college starts.

But you were supposed to come next fortnight?

Yeah, he looks sexy :P
What's his name?

Angira taps on the photograph once again to see the picture. She looks at the guy and waits for her text to get to Iona. She doesn't get a reply and leaves a few question marks with her message.

???

Then suddenly a message appears.

He is Ved Gulati.

Angira continues.

Now listen,
Tell me how to reach Bandra from Sakinaka.
I am staying here at Hotel Leela. Since you have been in Mumbai, you must be knowing things ;)

She gets a reply.

You can take an autorickshaw to Andheri Station.
And then take the local train till Bandra.
Or take a direct autorickshaw.

I have given you both the options :)

She writes.

Thanks a lot darling.
Let's catch up for coffee this weekend.

And the reply.

You're welcome.
This weekend I have my football match.
Please come to watch it at D.Y. Patil stadium, on Saturday, 4 p.m.

And don't just tell anyone where you stay without finding out more about them.

Angira is shocked to know she has texted a stranger. She enlarges the DP once more and texts back.

Who are you?

She gets the replies faster now.

I am Ved and I think you are mistaken.
It seems you have just come to Mumbai.
Welcome to Mumbai!

Angira gets angry. Thanks to her stupidity, she texted a complete stranger. And he replied without even knowing who she is.

Then why are we doing this time pass?
You could've told me earlier.

Then who would tell you how to reach Bandra from Sakinaka?

Angira reads the entire conversation again. She texts him trying to end the conversation. She is not at all interested in catching up with anyone.

Thanks.
All the best for your match.

No problem.
We are playing for an NGO this weekend. If you want you could come and contribute something.

It will be great.

Do you like watching football?

It's our human nature to be curious about hidden or unknown things. Angira replies.

Yes, I do watch football,
Even my cousin brother is a football player.
He plays for a club in Kolkata and they won a local championship last year.

The transmission of messages increases between them.

So you are from Kolkata?
I am also from Kolkata.

There's a loud voice coming from outside and the sound of the door opening. She walks out to find Charu standing at the door talking to someone. She returns to texting.

No, I am from Delhi.

What's your name?

Angira is still suspicious if this guy on WhatsApp is even real. She recalls what her mom had said before Angira had left for Mumbai. Her instinct to stay safe makes her block him later on WhatsApp. Though Angira is a kind person, she is quick at taking harsh steps when she senses something wrong. However, being kind-hearted as she is, she replies.

Angira.

So, you coming to watch my match?

Will ask my friend.

If she comes to watch your match, then so will I.
Thanks for the help. Need to go, bye.

Sure. You're welcome :) I'll wait. Or if you don't
want to come, at least buy few tickets.
It's for a good cause.

Charu closes the door.

'Who was at the door?' asks Angira, scrolling up the chat box and going through the whole conversation again.

'The room service guy.' Stretching her body, she asks. 'By the way, what's the matter? So busy texting.'

'Nothing, I was messaging Iona…' before Angira can complete the sentence, Charu interrupts, 'Oh, is she in Mumbai?'

'Don't know. So I was texting her and it went to someone else and imagine who that is?'

'A sexy guy or what?' Charu responds, winking at her.

'Yes, Ved. He is a football player. But I have never heard his name before.'

'Me neither. Maybe he's a local player. All footballers are not Messi,' Charu says.

'Hmm...but he told me that he is playing for some charity this weekend. So I'm not sure...'

Angira shows her his photo on WhatsApp where he is wearing a football jersey. Charu snatches the cellphone from her hand and looks at the photograph for some time.

'You got lucky, babes,' Charu says and continues, 'not bad. He looks fucking cute.'

Angira takes her cellphone back and says, 'What if this is his friend's picture? So you can't tell if he is fucking cute or a mofo.'

'Absolutely. That's what I wanted to tell you.'

Angira frowns at Charu and then asks , 'By the way, you want something to eat? I am ordering.'

'Oops...someone is being serious,' Charu says. 'By the way, what's this mofo and fofo you always talk about? I have been hearing these words for the last few weeks.'

Angira laughs, 'No baba, I am not serious. I got to know about this from Anushka. It's short for motherfucker and fatherfucker. Include it in your vocabulary. It will help here in Mumbai.'

They both laugh and enjoy their arrival in a new city, but who is Ved? They both are curious to know.

The Smart Loser

Ved is doing an MBA from SP Jain and he is a part of SPJFL, which is the SP Jain Football League. He has even joined a football institute where he spends most of his time. It's difficult for him to manage two institutes, but he is always up for a challenge and that's what sets him apart. That's the reason he is chasing his dream of playing for India someday. He is a football player before sunrise and after sunset, and an MBA student during the day. Nobody knows this except his teammates.

He has scored more goals than the number of days he has attended his MBA classes. He has cried, pleaded and begged in front of the faculty to excuse his poor attendance and allow him to appear for his exams. Though he has failed his exams several times, he has won the hearts of those at the football institute through sheer hard work and an undying passion for the game. He is doing an MBA for his mom's sake. During his engineering days, his friends used to call him Ctrl F Gulati. The reason behind this was in the four years of engineering, he faced disciplinary action thirteen times, each time because he was caught getting fucked. He was barred from playing in the university premises because he always failed in exams.

Today he is pumped up for the match at D.Y. Patil. Even though he is not expecting Angira to come, he is secretly hoping that she does. The attendance of each person matters to him, especially today because this is for a cause.

~

While Ved is getting ready for a warm-up session on the playground, Charu and Angira spend time together exploring the streets of Mumbai a couple of days before their college starts. They have dressed up like hipsters and are roaming around in Colaba Causeway. They expertly bargain with the owners of the fashion and jewellery huts spread across the place. No surprises. Indian girls are good at bargaining, especially girls from Delhi.

'So did you message him again?' Charu asks Angira while selecting a pair of red chandelier earrings.

'Who? Ved?' Angira asks.

Charu looks at her. 'No, Arjun. He was supposed to come with us, right?'

'Oh, he always has work. I messaged him in the morning but he had some work, so he didn't come. This looks nice on me, doesn't it?' Angira asks, pointing at a pair of ear cuffs embellished with red stones.

She tries them on and looks at herself in mirror. 'How's this?'

'Perfect, you look pretty in these. Take them.' Charu asks the shopkeeper to pack the earrings for Angira.

'And what about that guy Ved? Ved Gulati. That's the name, right?'

'Oh, that footballer? I blocked him on WhatsApp. Kitna bhaiya?' Angira takes her wallet out to pay the shopkeeper.

'₹370,' the guy replies and hands over the box to Angira.

'Why?' Charu asks Angira in a surprised tone.

'I can't trust anyone and talk to strangers just like that. We don't know anyone here and you know what guys are like these days na. Anyway, let's go, I am very hungry. I need to eat something,' Angira says, pointing at the stalls across the road.

'Yes, even I am hungry.'

'Let's have golgappas.'

'Well, you know we get the best golgappas in Connaught place,' Charu says, holding a paper bag in her hand.

'Sweetie, we can't go back to Delhi. So we need to have what we get here.'

They reach the counter and Angira asks the owner, 'Bhaiya, two plates of golgappe.'

'What?' the guy asks in confusion.

'Bhaiya, panipuri,' Charu repeats.

'Hmm,' the guy hands them two plates.

'They call it panipuri here.' She takes a piece from her plate and puts it in her mouth.

'You know what, we have finished our work, so we could go and watch his match. You shouldn't block him without knowing what he is like,' Charu advises Angira as they walk towards the roadside to take an autorickshaw.

'I'll give you his number and you can talk to him. Thirty-six guys are ready to follow us around in Delhi. If I was so interested in boys, I would have agreed to go out on a date with one of those guys in Delhi.'

'Are they all footballers?' Charu laughs and gives her a side hug. 'I was just joking. We both like watching football, so let's just go for fun and we'll get to take a look at Ved Gulati,' she says while crossing the road with Angira.

'Are you sure?' Angira asks in confusion. Still unsure, she leaves the decision to Charu. As it is they both are free to roam around today because from Monday their semester begins.

'C'mon we are going to watch the match, not him. Not the entire time anyway. Just chill. And anyway it's for some charity, right? So we are doing this for charity, not for him.'

Charu doesn't want to go back home so soon. She's excited to explore the street food of Mumbai.

'But the match is today at 4 p.m.,' Angira says, checking her cellphone.

'Should I unblock him to confirm the time?' she asks Charu.

'No, don't do that. At which stadium is the match being held?' Angira checks her WhatsApp.

'D.Y. Patil. But it's far away from here and it's already 3 o'clock.' Angira looks at Charu waiting for her decision.

'What about tickets?' Charu enquires.

'That we'll get anyway. If not we can always get them in black,' Angira says remembering her experience in Delhi during the Commonwealth Games.

'Are you sure?' Charu asks again.

'Yes, I have done this in Delhi several times during big events. We live in a country where we need to bribe the peon to get to a government officer. We break the signal and then give hundred rupees to the traffic police and drive off. So money wins over rules, babes. Getting a ticket in black is not that difficult. Let's go,' Angira says.

'Those police have taken 50-50 rupees from me in Delhi and I spent three years without a licence,' Charu says and they both laugh.

'Seriously.'

'Listen, if we want to get there on time we've got to take the Mumbai local to Nerul,' Charu says while checking train routes on google maps.

⁂

They get tickets easily upon reaching the stadium after standing in a queue for a few minutes.

'Looks like very few people have come to watch the match,' Charu says as they walk to the entry gate.

The moment they enter the stadium, they are immediately taken aback by the vibrancy of the place. Spectators are dressed in colourful clothes and everyone is cheering for the teams. There's an aroma of savoury snacks in the air. As soon as the ball reaches close to the goal post, the spectators shriek with joy.

'There's only thirty minutes left for the game to end and I don't even know the teams that are playing.' Angira tries to navigate through the jostling crowd to get some seats at the lower deck.

They manage to push through the crowds somehow.

'So it's Mumbai Warriors in blue and Kolkata United in white. Look at the scoreboard,' Charu shouts over the crowd and points towards the scoreboard so that Angira can understand her.

'Yes, seems so,' Angira says, reaching the desired seat in the fifth row from the ground. Charu follows her.

'Where is he?' Charu asks loudly.

'I don't know I can't see him. I mean, I can't recognize him.' Angira is observing each player from one goalpost to the other and suddenly spots a familiar face. 'Look, I think that is the guy,' she exclaims, giving away the fact that she was really excited to meet him.

'Is it the guy in the white jersey?' Charu enquires and tries to find out the name on his jersey.

The player reaches near the goalpost which is nearer to their seats and they finally see the name Ved printed on the back of his shirt.

'Yes, he is Ved Gulati. But he is losing every goal.'

Ved's disappointment at being unable to score a single goal is more than apparent. He angrily kicks his opponent and the referee gives him a warning, followed by a yellow card.

'He is not even trying,' Angira says, equally disappointed.

'Look who's so tense,' Charu teases her.

He makes another go at the goalpost and loses again. He is soon substituted by another player. The crowd keeps getting louder in anticipation of another goal. There is a rumour that the winning team could be mentored by Sourav Ganguly to play in a national league. In the last ten minutes Mumbai Warriors level the score at 2-2. Though Ved is a stranger to them, the girls root for Kolkata United. The match soon goes into overtime. The crowd is getting impatient hoping for Mumbai to score another goal. Soon Mumbai Warriors scores another goal. The local team finally wins the match 3-2. People discuss the strategy failures of the Kolkata team as the crowd slowly disperses.

'We came here to watch his match and he lost just like this,' Angira says as if it was she who sponsored the team.

'Baby, it's okay. At least we found the real Ved,' Charu grins and winks at her.

Angira nods in agreement.

'But I didn't like his game, the way he played. He could at least pass the ball to others closer to the goalpost. He wasn't even passing it to others. It's not a one-man game. Moreover, he kicked his opponent. I can still recall the expression on his face,' Angira says, and they both burst out laughing. They take the exit but choose a longer route to go home, because they aren't ready to call it a night yet.

Getting to Know Mr and Ms

The following morning is a lazy one. Angira is rolling around on her bed while Charu fiddles with pots and pans in the kitchen.

'Wake up, Angy! It is 10 a.m.,' Charu calls out to Angira as she walks towards her room.

Angira doesn't respond. Instead she takes her phone out from under the pillow and checks the messages on WhatsApp. She remembers that she had blocked Ved, so she unblocks him and decides to send him a text.

I came to watch your match yesterday with my friend.
For how many years have you been playing football?

Angira understands football quite well and had high expectations from him as a player. She had seen the intensity in his eyes. However, her opinion changed once she saw him playing yesterday. Ved replies immediately.

Thanks for coming.
I know I didn't play well.
Hopefully next time we'll win the match.

You were not even passing the ball to your mates.
It's not a one-man game, buddy.
Anyway, it's your game,
I was just a spectator and...

As she is about to send her reply, her phone rings. It's her mom. She cuts the call.

Busy???

She quickly types a reply.

Have to speak with mom, talk to you later. Bye.

Angira finishes the call with her mom when Charu enters the room.

While keeping her stuff in Angira's cupboard, Charu says, 'By the way, I was checking your Ved's profile on the internet. Did you talk to him again? When are you meeting him? Where does he live?'

'You ask so many questions. God! Stop Charu! You are such an askhole,' Angira says with a smile.

Amused, Charu asks, 'Now what's that?'

'A person who keeps questioning or asks for advice incessantly.'

'Then we both are askholes. I like it,' she says, still giggling. 'I am not joking. Why don't you talk to him? At least talk to Arjun. You know good people here in Mumbai. Anyway, let's roam around the city, we won't get the time later.'

'Shut up. I don't want to trouble him,' Angira answers with a frown.

'Trouble can turn into something more as well,' Charu teases her.

'Go away, idiot!' Angira laughs this time and mocks her back. 'And that won't ever happen.'

'What if it does?' Charu asks something which makes her blush. 'Why are you blushing so much?'

'Am I blushing? Am I?' Angira pushes Charu away by kicking her butt.

'Are you hiding something? Late last night you were chatting with someone,' Charu says, sounding suspicious.

'Nothing. No one. I just blush easily. By the way, I look sexier in the morning, isn't it?' Angira laughs and looks at herself in the mirror.

She gets out of bed in a pair of shorts and a t-shirt and walks into the hall. Her hair is untidy and her t-shirt seems a size too small. Charu pours some orange juice into two glasses and lays out the table for breakfast.

'I know you are hiding something,' Charu insists, certain that

Angira was sending messages to Ved earlier.

'Ved and I chatted. Just the usual. And I had to tell him that he should not play like that, even if it's for charity.'

'Ahem, ahem...someone has started chatting,' Charu teases her.

'Oh really,' Angira says, hoping to end the conversation right there.

'Yes, isn't it?' Charu claims.

Angira ignores her and takes a large sip of the orange juice.

'Let's talk about why *you* are still single?' Angira says and throws a paper ball at her.

'Now let's not go there. I was in a relationship for three years and I left him because he was a jerk. It's not as if I have been living in a cave you know,' Charu catches the ball and throws it back to her at a higher velocity.

'Oh, my princess!' Angira blows a kiss her way to diffuse the tension.

'By the way, players and celebrities are players in real life too.'

What Charu says plants a doubt in Angira's mind and the conversation inevitably leads back to Ved.

'Debatable notion,' replies Angira.

Once a thought takes root in your mind, no matter how hard you try, you are bound to be dragged back to it by stray doubts and questions till you become over conscious of it all. Angira just got to know about Ved a little more over chat and then Charu dropped that strange question. Whatever Angira expected of Ved, just the opposite has turned out to be true so far.

'But he seems like a good guy,' Angira defends him. She herself doesn't know why she has said this. Maybe she has just seen the one side of him, and the other will be better. Or will it be worse?

'Are you taking his side?' Charu questions her.

'No, I am just stating the facts. Anyway, do you want to take a shower? We need to go out soon,' she asks Charu.

'Yes, going,' pulling the towel off the dining table chair, Charu goes to the washroom and Angira gets back to work.

'Do talk to him and hang out with him, but don't trust people so easily that they can hurt you,' Charu warns her.

~

As Angira remembers her past, she decides to text Arjun. She finds comfort in his advice.

Hey!

Hey!
How are you?
How's life going in the new city?

Life is going good.
Are you free this weekend?

Not sure.
I'll let you know.

That means no :)
So, how's life?

It's nothing like that.
I'll message you.

Life is fucking crazy these days. I lost my luggage in Delhi.
And those asses didn't even lodge my FIR.
Hope you are enjoying :)

While Angira types a message to Arjun asking him to meet her over the weekend, a call from Ved flashes on her phone. She disconnects and writes to Arjun.

Oh shit. Did you tell papa?

I had a talk with Aunty.
Don't worry. I'll figure something out.
Need to go for now. See you :)

Sure. Take care of yourself.

Thanks!

She calls Ved back as she had earlier disconnected his call.

'Hey, how are you?' Angira asks.

'I am good, hope you are doing well,' Ved says, the enthusiasm in his voice all too apparent.

'How's your preparation going for the next match? When is it by the way? Actually I was on a call with Mom, so didn't reply to your message,' she tells him.

She feels guilty now for having blocked him on WhatsApp and is polite to him throughout the conversation.

'Which question do I answer first?' he replies and giggles.

'You can begin by answering how you are doing?'

They both smile. Everything starts with a smile

'I am perfectly fine, thank you,' Ved says. 'So what do you do?' he asks, breaking the ice.

'I am a student at NIFT,' she answers.

'So is there any specific reason for you to have picked NIFT?' he asks.

'NIFT Mumbai? Well, the presence of glamour and fashion in this city is undeniable. All the big fashion brands and retail houses are here. It's the ideal environment for fashion students in terms of industry exposure, class room learning, projects and placements.And what do you do apart from playing football?' Angira asks assuming he must be a student too.

'I am associated with the Indian Football School and I am doing an MBA from S.P. Jain Institute of Management and Research,' Ved replies.

'How did you get into the college? Even my cousin didn't get in.'

Ved wonders if that is a compliment or a judgement.

'I didn't get in on any lucky draw. I scored a ninety-five percentile in CAT this year,' he replies.

Angira sees Charu coming out of the bathroom.

'I'll call you after some time. Need to go for some urgent work. Bye.'

'Did I say something wrong?' he wonders. First impression is the last impression.

'What happened?' he asks her.

'Nothing. Just got some work,' Angira says.

Ved pauses for a second, anxious that he may have upset her and replies,

'Sure. Bye.'

Mr

Charu comes into Angira's room, refreshed after having taken a shower.

'Who were you talking to?'

'Mom. Arjun lost his luggage at Delhi station and Delhi Police refuses to file a case. So Mom is thinking of complaining about them,' Angira says, taking out her clothes and towel to go take a shower. She decides not to mention Ved, else Charu will start with her Dos and Don'ts. Instead she talks about Arjun.

'Like a complaint will help. The police will anyway sit on their ass and do nothing. So where is he now?'

'Reached Mumbai I guess.' Angira checks her cellphone while talking to Charu.

'So did you tell Aunty that you are meeting Arjun?' asks Charu

'I see you are a little more excited to meet Arjun than I am. Do you like him?' Angira teases her lightly.

'Of course I like him. I am not like you, who takes so much time to select things. Writers are romantic and very good in bed too,' Charu shouts from the other room.

'Oh really, what makes you say that?' Angira chuckles. 'Do you have any experience in this area?'

'Everything can't be told,' Charu sniggers confidently, applying lotion all over her body.

'Then stop dreaming, he can't be yours,' Angira says offhandedly.

Lost in her thoughts of Ved, Angira keeps her phone on the dining table and goes in for a shower. Though Charu is her best friend, Angira thinks it's best not to tell her about her chats with Ved. Charu will be the first one to know if anything happens, but Angira is not comfortable with the idea of sharing anything at this point.

Angira's cellphone rings while she's in the shower. At first Charu ignores it, but as it vibrates constantly, she cranes her neck back and shouts, 'Angira, your phone is ringing!'

'Okay,' Angira shouts from the bathroom. 'Who is it?'

'Someone named hash (#) is calling,' Charu says.

'Oh!' Angira exclaims and rushes to open the door of the bathroom in case she is inaudible. 'Leave that! I'll call later,' Angira says, reaching the table and shutting the phone.

'Why would you save a number with a hash symbol?' Charu asks her offhandedly.

'It comes on the top in the call-list and WhatsApp. Easy to manage, you know,' she answers.

ꟹ

The next day they rush to college, excited to meet new people and make new friends.

Walking to the classroom via the lobby, Angira says, 'I have the worst record when it comes to reaching class on time.'

'What are your names?' the person at the entry point asks with a big smile.

Charu looks at Angira, 'I told you not to take so much time in the shower.'

'You took more than an hour while getting ready,' replies Angira.

'But I got ready before you,' Charu hisses.

'Wait,' says the person at the entry point.

They both smirk looking at him.

'Can you both hear me?' he asks again.

The class sniggers at the scene.

'Don't laugh at them, tomorrow this could be you,' he says, offering them a seat in the class.

'What are your names?'

'Sir, Angira.'

'Charu, sir.' She gives a fake smile while answering.

'Sir Angira and Charu Sir,' he tries to crack a joke but nobody laughs this time.

'Angira and Charu,' he says again and they both smile and reply 'Yes.' Then they utter under their breaths, 'And you are an asshole.'

Once they settle down, Mr Alberto continues with the lecture on the 'Introduction of Contextual Design Studies and Communication'. Charu is attentive, taking down copious notes while Angira, clearly bored, takes her phone out and messages Ved.

Hey!

Hi.

While waiting for Ved's reply, she messages few of her friends who are studying in different cities.

'What are you doing? He will kick us out of the class if he sees you,' Charu says.

'This asshole? No, he won't.' Angira keeps her cellphone on the desk, which is easily hidden by the tall classmate sitting in front of her.

'This is the advantage of sitting in the back row. Nobody can see us, but we have a clear view of everyone. From today we'll sit here only.' Angira looks at her phone and gets engrossed in typing messages on WhatsApp. Her eyes are on the white board, but her fingers are clicking away on the keypad.

So how's it going?

As of now, nothing is going good.
I have an internal test,
And I have been warned not to appear for exams.

Oh that's fun :B
Low attendance?

Yeah

So Ved Gulati is a Satyavadi Harishchandra
who can't get proxies?

Ved is reminded of his engineering college days where he had friends who cared, who would give proxies on his behalf.

Ved gets out of his bed and walks towards the balcony. The cold breeze rushes towards him; a feeling of gentle bliss spreads over him. He breathes in the calm.

My friends tried to but they were caught,
And that's the reason I have been warned.
By the way all Gandhians are not like me.
They are busy with women empowerment :P
LOL
What's up with you?

Nothing, first day in class.

So how's it going?

Not so good actually.
We were late for class
And he cracked a joke on us
In front of everyone.
Now we are sitting in the last row.

Oh that's fun ;)

Don't use my lines on me.

Just wanted to make you feel, you know...
How does it feel ;)
Chill,
Class means Come Late And Start Sleeping

LOL, you are mad. So what else?

Prof. Alberto looks at Angira who promptly looks alert, but her fingers still run on the touchpad.

Nothing. Will go to class and then prepare for exams.
From next week, match practice will begin.
You can come if you want.

Ved invites her to watch his match because he is feeling a little more confident about this game and is sure he will impress her.

Dude, your match...Noooo,
can't take the risk ;)

Multiple Os always have a positive meaning. Okay, come if you're free :)

She doesn't want to sound rude.

Will see.

Eventually, she agrees to come for his football session after he convinces her.

Okay. Well one advice for you, rather than sitting in the back row, you should sit in the first row.

There are a few advantages—you can learn whenever you want and sleep whenever you feel like because nobody pays attention to the first row.

Their eyes always seek answers from people sitting in the middle and the back row.

Try it. It worked for me in my four years of engineering and still works in my MBA classes.

Angira smiles at his reply. She thinks he is quite cool. But whenever she feels this way about anyone, Charu tries to change her mind by insisting that people are different from what they make themselves out to be on chat or over a call. Charu believes that the truth lies behind the camera and not in front of it.

Dude, fashion designing can be understood sitting miles away from the faculty, but MBA can't be done like that.

You need to focus on the formulae and graphs of Demand and Supply.

Yes, but I don't want to live a boring life. I am either playing a game or studying. Life should be exciting every day.

His logic impresses Angira. Charu's eyes fall on the phone and she excitedly asks if it is Ved. On getting the confirmation she smiles.

'All the best,' Charu shows a thumbs up and winks.

Angira types a message to Ved.

You have given me so much 'guru gyan', now I'll give you the 'guru mantra' to pass your exams.

Before going for exams, write all the tough formulae on the scale. It won't be visible until you place it against a white background which is your answer sheet.

You can also use your scientific calculator or its cover to write whatever you want.

That gives you enough space to write and it is not visible until it's held up against light.

These two ideas will surely work and nobody would have any evidence to catch you.

You are a player; you must play the game safely ;)

Ved smiles on reading the text and now he actually wants to meet her. She has a good sense of humour. He types a message and pop, a notification appears on top. Angira taps on that.

Send me your photograph.
If you don't mind.

Why do you want my picture?

No, just felt like seeing you.

Then don't feel too much.

☺

'But there is always a tomorrow,' he thinks and types again.

Don't tell me,
You haven't checked my profile on Facebook.

Not yet.

I have other work to do as well.
I would have surely checked had you won that day.
But you disappointed me.

I know.
Now don't depress me.

Lol, okay.

Please come if you can. Will try not to disappoint you this time.

Ved lies in bed, constantly thinking of Angira and what she must look like. He begins downloading her profile picture. He is optimistic and hence chooses to be happy with what he has in life. For now he might not have a proper picture, but he is nevertheless quite excited about his interaction with Angira. Her picture finally appears.

She has dark brown hair, parted to the side. It covers an eye and a side of her forehead. She has finely sketched eye brows. Her whitish skins glows and there's a twinkle in her eyes.

She looks beautiful in the picture.

'What are you doing? You haven't even met her and you're already staring at her lips,' Ved's notorious mind asks him.

'Her lips are beautiful and there is nothing wrong with looking at them,' his heart answers back.

'Indeed her lips,' are fine and kissable,' his mind replies. He feels awkward for a moment, but soon types out a message.

Nice DP.
You work for some NGO?

Yes, I do from time to time.
I just try to spread a little happiness.

Her words make him smile. He wants to continue the chat, but he has to rush and before he's about to explain it to her, someone knocks on his door unexpectedly.

Bye. See you later.

Bye.

Ved soon leaves for college because he has been called regarding his low attendance.

He tries to come up with new excuses which he hasn't used before, anything to help him get back to playing football.

Expecting the Unexpected

The clock indicates it is 8.30 p.m. Just like any other day, Ved reaches home covered in sweat. He switches on the TV and keeps pressing the button until a sports channel appears. He gets up from the sofa and goes to the kitchen to get a glass of juice. Taking sips of it, Ved checks his WhatsApp. One of his friends had messaged him about tomorrow's surprise test, which is not a surprise anymore. Few of his friends are in good terms with Mr Subramaniam. Meeting faculties in their cabin always helps stay a step ahead.

His positive nature makes Ved everyone's favourite. He is loved by everyone and all his friends are very supportive of him. One moment, Ved feels that he shoudn't give a damn about his MBA, that he should just leave everything and concentrate only on football. The next moment he is not so sure if he will do well as a player in the long run. He is confident about his game, but he is worried about the lack of opportunities and exposure in the field of sports in general. Hence, the MBA is his backup plan. Sometimes, it's like the MBA is his part-time course and football is his full-time passion.

'Who is it?' Ved asks while sitting up on his sofa.

'Hey, it's me,' comes a voice from outside.

'Who's this?' he enquires again just to trouble him, though he knows who is there on the other side.

'Your grandfather,' the voice replies, mildly irritated. Ved laughs at the response and opens the door. It's Arjun.

Arjun and Ved have been living together for the last few months. Arjun, Anushka and Ved used to study in the same college. They both came to Mumbai as engineers, but Ved couldn't keep up with his 'job'. Actually he did not want to keep up with them either. They were good friends in college, but after college everyone got busy with their lives. They were not in touch for several years. Just two months before Ved started looking for a place to live, Arjun landed up in Mumbai.

Anushka happened to know that they both were looking for a place and suggested that they move in together. So they rekindled their friendship, but could never rekindle the bond they shared in college.

What if Ved, Arjun and Angira run into each other at the same time? Nobody is aware of the fact that Ved and Arjun are flatmates other than Anushka.

Arjun does not share his dreams with anyone. Revelling in mystery, he still manages to be a people's person. These days he has tremendous work pressure, so sometimes he gets frustrated with the way Ved lives in the house.

'You didn't go to office?' Ved enquires.

'I went day before yesterday,' he says and throws his bag on the sofa.

'You mean, you didn't come home last night?' Ved asks him, surprised.

'Had some work. So had to finish it off,' Arjun manages a smile despite being exhausted after his hectic work-day.

'Ved, why don't you clean your room, it's so messy,' Arjun tells him, inspecting the rooms. Sometimes they have arguments because Ved is not as responsible as Arjun.

'It's not fair,' Arjun goes to the washroom, his tone is gruff and he is in a bad mood.

'You were not at home yesterday?' Ved asks him again.

Arjun ignores the question.

'Why don't you leave your 9 to 6 office. It just looks like 69 but doesn't give any pleasure at all, does it?'

'Not everything in life is about pleasure, Ved,' Arjun finally snaps.

'We're obviously very different from each other,' Ved shouts.

'Yes we are, but I am not going to marry you,' Arjun responds.

'Fuck off!' Ved again shouts, loud and clear, smiling at the silliness of their lives and how they preserve their innocent college banter to this day. Ved always tries to cheer him up, but he also knows that there are some things that Arjun never talks about.

Arjun comes out of washroom. It is then that Ved asks suspiciously, 'Why do you have this red mark on your neck? Who gave it to you? Is it a love bite?'

Arjun disregards the question and goes in his room.

'What happened? I am talking to you,' Ved asks him again.

'Nothing. By the way, why don't you tell me about the frequent beeps on your phone? I have noticed it has increased over the last fortnight.'

'We need to talk,' Ved says, stepping into Arjun's room.

'Yes, tell me.'

'You haven't been talking to me properly for the past two months. If anything has happened, please share it with me. I'll try my best to help you,' Ved wants to know why Arjun has been so serious lately.

'Ved, I am not your girlfriend that I have to share everything with you. Nothing happened. Things are not like they were when we were in college. We are friends, even good friends I'd say, but I go to office, I have work. It's difficult for me to manage everything. You understand that, right?'

'Yes, I do. Sorry for troubling you. Hope someday we'll share the same bond like we used to,' Ved goes back to his room and starts cleaning up the mess around. He is hurt, but he understands that Arjun has no time for himself or for Ved. However, Ved feels that there's more to it than just that.

'By the way, Anushka called today,' Ved informs him.

'What did she say?' Arjun enquires.

'She tried your number but your phone was switched off, so she called me to ask where you were.'

'Okay, my cellphone's been acting weird lately,' Arjun says. 'So what's going on with you these days?' he asks, trying to lighten up the mood.

Ved is about to say something, but he suddenly stops.

'Nothing. I need to take a shower.' Ved searches through his notes from the heap of books. He continues, 'Arjun, call Anushka. She told me to inform you to call her.'

'Okay,' Arjun says and walks away.

Ved answers his ringing cellphone. 'Hello!'

'Hey, how are you?' Angira asks, while Ved is still struggling to wrap his head around the concept of Demand and Supply, and its elasticity factor 'e'.

He says cheerfully, 'I am good, how's your college going? You must have gotten used to the morning schedule by now.' Ved keeps the pencil in between the book and closes it.

'Yes, it's alright, so many new things to learn. I'm quite busy actually. One of my aunties has even asked me to tailor things for her,' says Angira.

She continues, 'Well, you say, how are your exams going? Today must be your last one, right? I didn't call you all this while because I figured you'd be busy studying.'

'So far, I'll be able to pass the exams. Your advice is definitely working. It has helped me like a straw helps a drowning man. By the way these aren't exams, they are sessional tests and tomorrow there is one more surprise test.' Ved gets up and goes to the corner of the room where he keeps his football and other stuff.

He looks out of the window. He takes the football in his hand and spins it on one finger.

'Are you serious?' she is surprised. 'I can't believe you are using those tricks. I was joking.'

Without wavering, Ved answers, 'Yes, I need to pass these exams, otherwise I won't be able to go for team selection in Kolkata next month. I have to pass them anyhow.'

'Okay, you'll pass don't worry,' Angira assures him. 'Ved, I have a question for you.'

'Yes, please.'

'Why are you doing an MBA when football means the world to you?' She asks something that Ved has never discussed with anyone.

'Everybody wants to be an employed citizen in this country of unemployment,' he answers, hoping to change the topic.

'No, I mean seriously, why?' Angira asks again, her voice reflecting her determination.

'I'll tell you everything someday. It is a long story.'

'I don't understand one thing. We have a population of 1.3 billion and it's still increasing. Then why don't we have a good national football team?' she asks the million dollar question.

'That is something only our Prime Minister can answer. Games like cricket get all the exposure, though I like cricket too. I am hoping one day we'll be representing India in the FIFA World Cup.'

He believes that success comes to those who start from the scratch and before he closes his eyes forever, he wants to play for India at an international level.

'Well, after my exams I have to go shopping for some shirts and other football stuff. So if you are free next weekend, I'd like to tell you more about my fabulous life as a footballer,' he says, clearly wanting to meet her.

He is not looking for romance but wants to meet someone he can share his feelings with. He is attracted to her and gets a positive vibe from her.

'Not sure. I'd like to meet but I need to check if my roommate Charu can join us,' Angira says.

'You ask your roommate for everything?' Ved jeers.

Suddenly he hears a second phone call from Angira's side.

'Mom is calling, will catch you later. Bye. See you,' she says and disconnects the call.

Ved takes a deep breath and awaits Angira's reply about meeting with him.

Not an Official Date

Finally, the day Ved and Angira are to meet arrives. He plans on asking her to meet him at Bandstand. With the raging sea on one side and the glamorous Bandra on the other, it is the ideal place for a romance like theirs to bloom. But he must first consider if she would like to meet at such a place. Would she prefer a coffee shop by the sea or is there another place which is perhaps more convenient for her? Having taken his time to consider everything, he asks her to come to Juhu beach where they could enjoy a walk on the beach, take in the sea breeze and really get to know each other. Perhaps later she could help him shop for clothes in Bandra.

The next morning Ved shoots a text to Angira, inviting her to the beach. While he is excited at the prospect of meeting her, a part of him is also on the edge. He has not been on a date since college and though he understands this is not a date, he knows there is a possibility of things moving beyond the phase of being just friends.

Ved chooses his clothes meticulously. He wears his favourite white cotton shirt. It fits his sculpted sporty physique well. He wears this shirt at events which are important, teaming it up with a blue blazer. Today, however, knowing it will be a fairly hot and humid evening, he chooses to ditch the blazer. He opens the top button of his shirt—an effect which gives a little peek at his well-built, muscular chest.

He has a light stubble which gives him a rugged look. Ved is a little conscious knowing that Angira is from the northern part of India and perhaps expects a little more from the boys she chooses to meet. He is not sure he wants to impress her, but he surely wants to look as good as he does in his Whatsapp photo.

He calls Angira. 'Are you coming?'

'Hey, I'm sorry I forgot to tell you. I am stuck with some work and it will take some time. Can we meet next weekend? I was just about to call you, but I completely forgot. I am with Charu. I'll call you once I reach home,' she says looking at Charu, who is buying some household items. Charu stares at her, curious to know who she was talking to.

Ved walks out of his room sluggishly and replies, 'No worries. Have fun.'

He does not express any anger towards her for not telling him about her plans earlier.

❧

Rather sad, Ved walks into his room, hoping to avoid unnecessary questions from Arjun.

'Hey, are you going somewhere?' Arjun asks while entering his room.

'No, was just going for shopping with friends. Do you want to come?' Ved asks him.

'No, carry on. Wait, I've got something for you,' Arjun says, handing him an envelope. Ved absentmindedly takes the envelope from his hand but doesn't open it.

'What is this?' Ved assumes it's a letter regarding his team selection process for Kolkata.

'Don't know. Open it. I just received it from the guard downstairs,' Arjun says. Ved tears the envelope evenly from one side, excited to read the contents of the letter.

> To,
> Mr Ved Gulati,
> Date: 22 June 2015
>
> Subject: Letter for property transfer
>
> Dear Mr Ved Gulati,
>
> I am hereby writing this letter in continuation to our discussion regarding the property of Late Shri Devdatta Gulati. On completion of the formalities pertaining to the transfer of rights, the court hereby transfers the rights to the property on your name in all respects.

A tear drops on the letter. Ved wipes his eyes. Arjun gets worried and takes the letter from his hand.

'What happened? What is this, Ved?' he asks handing back the letter to him.

'Now I can find a good guy for my sister,' he says.

His priority is getting his little sister married and he is happy that he can finally make it happen.

'There was some property issue since the past few years that I had told you about. My uncle took everything when my grandmother passed away. But finally the court has resolved the issue and we got our rightful part of the property. Now everything will be fine.'

'That's such great news!' Arjun pats Ved on his back and they hug each other.

'Dude, don't cry, it's good news. I am happy for you,' says Arjun.

Ved's phone rings.

'Your phone. It's ringing,' Arjun says.

He takes his cellphone from his pocket and comes out in the hall to answer the call. Once the call ends, he rushes back to the room. He sprays some perfume, sets his hair again and dashes back to the hall.

'Arjun, see you in the evening. We can party once I am back!'

Arjun reads the letter that Ved left on his bed. That reminds him of the days when he and his family had to face the worst after his grandfather gave nothing to his family and both his uncles took everything. He wouldn't wish the same on anyone else and is glad that Ved and his family got out of that situation.

❧

There are no words to express Ved's happiness today. He calls her while taking an autorickshaw to Juhu.

'I knew you were coming.'

'No, I wasn't. Charu and I had to buy some stuff,' Angira says.

'Okay, you could have bought them with me,' he replies.

'It was some personal stuff.'

'Okay,' Ved does not probe further.

'Actually we had to get some groceries from the supermarket.

Now I am reaching home and will leave for Juhu beach in a bit. At what time will you be reaching?'

'I will reach in about fifty to fifty-five minutes,' he says.

Ved knows girls take some time even if they are ready. So he adds fifteen minutes to give her that extra breathing space.

'Are you coming from Mars?'

'No, that takes more time than what is expected here,' he answers.

'Shut up.'

'So are you excited?' he asks.

'Excited for what? Dude, I am not coming for a date, I am coming to help you. Who knows, when you become a famous player someday, I can tell people that I helped you shop,' Angira says.

Ved is happy that she dropped a hint of a long-term friendship blossoming between them.

'So are you being selfish?' he asks her.

'Of course,' she mocks him.

'This is going to be a good day,' he says. 'Okay, so leave soon and give me a call once you reach.'

'Sure.'

'Okay, bye.'

Once the call ends, he texts her on WhatsApp.

This is going to sound very filmy, but
I must say you are lucky for me.

Glad to hear that.
But what's the reason for this compliment?

Will tell you once we meet.
Come soon.

'Why do we text someone when we have just finished talking to them? Is this a sign of affection? Or is it just infatuation which will vanish in a few weeks?' Ved's mind is full of questions to which he can never find the answers.

And so It Begins

Angira is waiting for the metro at the D. N. Nagar metro station. She softly pinches her cheeks to make them blush. She boards the train and takes a seat. On hearing the announcement for the desired station, she walks out of the metro exit to take an auto to Juhu Beach. As July is here, monsoons have begun full-swing in Mumbai. The sky is cloudy and dark. While she is concerned about the impending illness if she were to get wet, for once she chooses to enjoy the weather instead of cursing herself for not bringing an umbrella.

It being a weekend, the beach is crowded. People are enjoying the weather, relaxing and spending time with their loved ones. Usually, Angira comes to this place for a walk whenever she feels like spending some time alone. She shares a special bond with nature and feels elated when the waves touch her feet. She loves getting wet in the rain, so part of her is glad that she forgot to carry an umbrella today. The simple joys of life. When she gets to the beach she doesn't even care if Ved is coming to meet her. She walks on the promenade along the sea from one end to the other. The air is so refreshing and pleasant.

Her phone rings. It's Ved.

'Hey, I reached fifteen minutes ago. Where are you?'

'I am just reaching in five minutes, in an auto right now,' Ved says. Angira can easily hear the roadside noise.

Ved has already brought chocolates for Angira. This is something he has learnt from Arjun. If one is late, chocolates always seem to pacify them, especially girls because they generally hate to be kept waiting.

'Does this always happen or are you intentionally late today?' Angira sneers at him.

'I'd like to ask you this question someday when you're stuck in traffic,' he says.

'Okay, I rest my case. Sometimes you get so serious,' she says.

Ved was not stuck anywhere in traffic. He got late while buying chocolates for her.

'Sometimes it's good to lie as long as you don't get caught,' Ved thinks as the autorickshaw reaches Juhu beach.

∽

After sundown, everyone seems to head for the beach to get some fresh air. The sea inadvertently becomes a passive listener to people walking along the beach. A long walk along the beach helps one reflect on all that life has thrown at them. Many people just sit along the way and relax. Kids are enjoying playing in the sand.

Angira comes here to observe people. It inspires her work in fashion. She watches their expressions, how they interact with each other, their response to the endless sea before them; it helps her derive some creative ideas which eventually translate into her designs.

Ved reaches and pays the autorickshaw driver.

He pauses to thinks about some significant moments he has spent at this very spot. In an otherwise hectic life, this place provides him some much-needed solace. He looks far into the sea, and then in a split second, it starts to rain. He runs towards the famous Pav Bhaji counters near the promenade.

Once under the shop's roof, he calls Angira. 'Hey, it's raining...'

Before he can say anything else, she says, 'Yeah, it's raining. Have you reached or still on the way?'

Her voice indicates that she is rushing to find some shelter from the rain.

'I have reached. I am standing here at the first pav bhaji counter when you enter the beach. Can you come here? We can wait here till it stops raining. I don't have an umbrella.'

'Sure, even I forgot to carry one. I think I see your stall. See you,' Angira says and disconnects the call.

The aroma of pav bhaji mingles with the smell of icecream in the air. Ved enjoys this brief moment of anticipation. It is worth waiting out here. He is a little nervous now. He looks at himself in the cellphone's screen and tries his best to set his hair, which seems impossible to do with the strong wind that's blowing in his direction. He looks for Angira in the crowd.

Angira reaches the counter and spots a guy standing outside, drinking water. He is wearing a white shirt and blue jeans, has a well built figure, and black intense eyes. A few raindrops from his hair are trickling down his neck. She wasn't expecting Ved to look like this. He is not just handsome and cool, but also stunning and hot. Her heart says this is Ved, but she just can't believe that she can be so lucky.

'Lucky for what?' she thinks.

'Nothing,' she answers her own question.

She tries not to stare at him, but the truth is, Angira is completely attracted to him from the get-go. Suddenly she starts to wonder if he finds her attractive. Ved turns around and spots Angira, immediately recognising her, but pretends that he hasn't seen her yet and walks to the other side. She isn't able to walk towards him easily because it's crowded.

She cranes her neck and shouts, 'Hey, Ved!'

She walks towards him.

'Hi, how are you?' says Ved, trying to sound a little louder than the chaos around them.

'I am good. How are you?' she asks.

Angira, always confident, never felt nervous meeting new people. However, today she is a little jumpy meeting Ved for the first time.

'I am good too. How long have you been waiting,' Ved asks.

'Twenty minutes. Yeah, you are late by twenty minutes,' she says, obviously miffed.

'Sorry to keep you waiting. So how's it going?' Ved steps aside to let a few people pass.

They both are standing next to each other, facing the sea. It is still raining out there.

'All is going well,' she gives a straight answer.

'Do you want some water?' he asks her.

'Yeah,' she takes a few sips.

'What's going on with you? And when are you going to Kolkata?' asks Angira and starts with some small talk to initiate the conversation.

The rain has slowed down. They walk towards a corner as people have started moving around.

'Maybe in two weeks, but I am still not sure. I am waiting for the confirmation letter.'

Ved wants to know more about her and there couldn't be a better topic than football to start that process.

'By the way, what do you like about football? Because in India nobody encourages football over cricket. Cricket is a religion in India.'

'Actually, I like the game because my cousin plays football and my family is a big fan of Messi. Now, what my mom likes in Messi that only my mom knows. However, I can say one thing for sure that we are one of the craziest Punjabi families in Delhi, who like to watch football with parathas and butter.'

'Do you want to eat pav bhaji?' Ved asks her, smiling.

He watched the cook chopping onions and lemons at the counter.

'Do you want to eat?' Angira asks him.

'Come, we'll eat some. This place is famous for its pav bhaji,' Ved approaches the pav bhaji counter.

'We have the best golgappe in Delhi that you can't beat at all,' she says, throwing her hair back.

'Golgappe?' Ved has never heard of it before.

'Oh, I mean pani puri. We call it golgappe in Delhi,' she says. She is reminded of the conversation Charu and she had at the golgappe counter on the day when they both went to watch Ved's football match.

Ved orders two plates of pav bhaji.

'Just take one plate. I won't have much,' Angira says. 'Bhaiya, one plate.'

'So tell me something about your family? Do they support you? They must be happy having a qualified, intelligent and smart football player in the family.' She realizes that she used one too many adjectives.

Ved is concentrating on the counter and doesn't answer her question. The server gives him the plate. The aroma of spices, lemon and onions is so heady and tempting that it's impossible to stand there without having a bite of it.

'You didn't answer...' Angira repeats, squeezing the piece of lemon and then sprinkling chopped onion over the bhaji.

'They are...' Ved avoids answering her question. 'So tell me about your family.'

'I have an older sister, Mom, Dad and me—hum do hamare do.'

They both giggle.

Soon it stops raining, except for a slight drizzle. Few people are still leaving their umbrella open, while some have preferred to close them and walk in the drizzle. The scent of earth after rain brings with it a sense of renewal.

'It's so amazing to walk in the rain, isn't it?' Angira asks, watching the people who are walking by.

'I have not experienced it yet,' Ved says gently and follows her eyes to look at the same people.

'Seriously?'

'Yes, I have never walked in the rain.' He takes the last bite of the food. 'But I have spent enough time over the years on the football ground on rainy days,' Ved says. He tries to find out if she wants to walk on the beach. He guesses so as Angira is new to Mumbai and these beaches are new for her.

Before he asks her, she asks him, 'Do you want to try?'

'Walk in the rain?' he asks.

'Yes.'

'Are you sure?' he confirms.

'Yeah, come.'

Why do all girls like extra lemon?

Why do all girls walk in the rain?

Why doesn't she know that it will ruin my shirt?

These questions come to his mind and before she says anything else, he says, 'No, that's fine.'

'Come, let's walk,' she finishes the last bite. She gives the plate to the cleaning person roaming around.

Ved doesn't want to go with her. He is afraid of telling her the truth. He feels he might come across as a self-obsessed person. He takes a moment to reply and prefers to speak the truth and not tell a lie.

'My shirt...' he is about to say and she understands.

'C'mon, shirts? You can buy them anytime but this moment will take another year to come back and maybe in Mumbai, never.'

Ved knows Angira is right. He thinks for a moment and decides to follow his heart.

'Okay,' he says, wiping his hand with a tissue.

They go down three flights of stairs and start walking on the beach.

Oh, the chocolates! They are still in my pocket, I forgot to give them to her.

He remains quiet for a moment and then decides to keep them in his pocket. By now they must have melted.

They walk along the beach, enjoying the fine rain. It is then that Ved realizes how enjoyable rain can be. Walking on the beach, he talks about his life. He is curious to know about her, so he asks her to talk about herself.

Angira talks about her family and her dreams. She shares her past experiences about love and life.

'I was also in a relationship in college. Those were the best days of my life, but he left me for someone else. That's the worst thing that happened to me but I survived, thanks to the support of my family. I lost three kilos in a month after the breakup and gained four kilos later,' Angira says. Though she's talking about something that deeply affected her in the past, she ends her sentence on a funny note.

Ved starts sniggering.

'Really.'

'Yes. It took a long time to understand that to be happy you must focus on what you have, which is far more important than what you don't,' she says.

She pauses, 'Just a minute.'

She folds her pants and a black anklet grabs Ved's attention.

While she is busy folding her pants, Ved, who's standing next to her, says, 'There is nothing wrong with falling or rising in love but be sure, that at the end of the day, you raise yourself in love.'

Angira just smiles looking at him and stands up.

They walk for some time and then sit by the sea.

The boy who was worried that his shirt will get wet and dirty is suddenly carefree and not thinking about anything else.

'Hey, I got this for you, as a safeguard against your anger at me getting late, but it has melted,' Ved takes the chocolate out of his pocket and gives it to her.

'That's okay,' she tears the wrapper and starts eating.

'So what do you have to shop for?' she enquires, still licking her lips.

'I can get the stuff next weekend. Actually, I'm still waiting for the letter. Till then I have enough time. We can go next weekend, if you are free.'

Ved doesn't want to lose an opportunity to meet her again. He is enjoying her company. Today, rather than spending time in a mall, he wants to spend time with her on the beach.

When the rains have stopped, Angira says, 'I am sorry if I dirtied your shirt.'

She looks innocent and endearing while saying this.

'No, that's fine, I'll wash it. Daag acche hain.' They have a hearty laugh.

'Wait, I'll get something to drink. I'm thirsty.' Ved goes to a hawker and gets a bottle of water.

Angira sits on the sand. Ved finishes half the water in one go and she uses the rest to wash her sandy ankles.

'So, have you ever been to Delhi?' she asks after taking a few sips of water.

'No, but if I pursue football and get selected for a team, I may go for a match over there to promote football.' Ved takes the empty bottle from her hand and throws it directly into the dustbin.

'Do you play basketball as well?' Angira asks.

'I tried but I am really bad at it. Why did you ask that? Do you?' Ved questions her.

'The way you threw the bottle into the dustbin,' she grins.

'Good observer,' he raises his eyebrows in salutation.

'I can be your instructor as well,' she says with a smile.

'Aha! Really?' he asks.

'Oh yes!' she winks in response.

Are you in love with her? His mind needs the answer right now.

'No, I am not, but I feel so happy spending time with her,' his heart responds.

A cold breeze is blowing and the sun has set. The weather is pleasant. They both do not want to go back, but it's getting late as Angira has to go out with Charu and some friends for dinner. By the time the clock strikes 8, they both say their goodbyes.

A Bag of Happy Cards

Love in our modern times is such that when someone special comes into our life, gadgets can define how close they really are to us. Ved has used some special characters to save Angira's number. A new symbol (^;^) is displaying these days in his recent call list. Angira has saved Ved's number with a hash symbol just to keep his number at the top on her contact list.

They both have started talking to each other about their days and even their secrets. They have spent more than two months getting to know each other. From good morning messages to late night calls, everything is evidently visible to Arjun but he doesn't know who Ved is involved with these days.

On 14th August, Angira turns twenty-six. A week before the big day, Ved is looking to confirm if Angira is going to Delhi to celebrate her birthday. In case she does not travel back home, Ved has already planned a special surprise for her. After a tiring game of football, he calls her to ask offhandedly about her birthday plans among other things

'Hey, what's up?' he asks cheerfully while panting a little.

'Hi, nothing much. I was just passing time watching television. Some kabaddi. By the way, what happened? Are you practising right now?' Angira presumes that he is playing football.

After days of talking, it's very easy for her to guess his activities. However, Charu is calling her, something Ved can hear over the call.

Ignoring the diversions, he asks, 'So someone in your family used to play Kabaddi?'

'Are you pulling my leg, Mr Gulati?'

'Just asking. Your cousin plays football, so I thought you also know someone who plays Kabaddi,' Ved says with a smile.

'No, I was just wiling away my time,' a jaded Angira retorts.

'Well someone has her birthday next week, right? So when are you going home?' Ved asks, pretending he doesn't know much about her plans.

'Yes but this is going to be a boring one,' she says ruefully, her voice down.

'Why? Are you not going home on your birthday?' Ved needs this answer so that he can execute the surprise he has planned.

'No, I have to submit a report and I have to be here as a few fashion shows are going to be held in Mumbai. So...'

'So where is the party?' he changes the topic not letting her guess his intentions.

Ved figures that she anyway won't guess what he is upto because she knows that he is not in the habit of surprising people.

'You want me to give you a treat? Are you sure? But for that a person should be physically present, and someone is very busy these days,' Angira says, mocking him.

They were supposed to meet this week, but Ved was busy so he couldn't make it to the venue and cancelled the plan at the last moment. Now he has to listen to her tirade until they meet again.

'No, I am free for you,' he flirts as he walks on the ground.

'Then we'll meet next weekend,' she says merrily.

'Sure. I will call you at night. I hope you'll be awake till then. I've got to go now,' Ved has utilized his time-out well. He runs to the centre of the ground thinking about ways to make her birthday memorable.

'Sure. Bye.'

∞

With one day to go for Angira's birthday, Ved opens his cupboard and takes out all the envelopes that he has been making since last week. Angira called him from Charu's phone a while ago as her phone was not working. This is how Ved gets Charu's number, something which allows his plans to work perfectly. He calls Charu.

'Are you home? Where is Angira?'

'Yes, I am home,' she says.

'Is Angira home?'

'She has gone for an event. What happened? Why are you being so impatient about her?' she asks bluntly.

Before she gets confused, Ved requests her to help him in executing his plan.

'No, tomorrow is her birthday, so I wanted to give her a surprise. I need your help in making it successful.'

Ooh, what have you planned for her?' she asks him eagerly.

'Don't tell her anything, please. Can we meet in the evening?' he asks her hoping she'll say yes.

Having listened to Angira talk about Ved, Charu has come to like him and agrees to help him.

'Okay. It sounds like a big surprise,' she agrees to meet him in the evening.

❧

In the evening, Ved reaches her apartment and knocks on the door. He has started figuring out the perfect plan and imagines how Angira will respond to the surprise. Ved knows that confidence comes from planning one's moves so the entire event runs smoothly.

'Hey,' a cheerful girl welcomes Ved with a broad smile.

This must be Charu, but why she is smiling so broadly? She should be nervous as she is meeting you for the first time.

Ved is a little jumpy. He hopes Angira does not come back early and his well thought-out plan goes for a toss. He has already reached her home so late. He hands over the bag to Charu and explains her a little about its contents, making Charu a part of the plan.

'You can come inside,' Charu says, showing the way to the hall.

'No, I'll leave now. I need to go,' Ved needs to rush after giving the bag and update Charu about what to do with it over the phone.

He knows the value of each second. However, he is also excited to check out the place where Angira lives. Though, virtually, he knows everything about this place as Angira has described it to him over the last two months of talking and meeting during evenings in the city.

'Doesn't look good, come,' Charu repeats.

Someone passes him on the stairs. In order to avoid being seen, he quickly goes inside the apartment and sits on a bean bag which seems like it hasn't been used for a long time.

'What do I do with these?' Charu asks, keeping the bag of envelops aside and offering him some water.

'I'll message you the instructions on WhatsApp?' Ved says.

'Okay,' she responds.

His eyes fall on the clothes hanging in the hall outside, which includes undergarments and a towel.

'So, are you guys dating?' she asks, adjusting herself on the other bean bag kept across the hall.

Charu notices Ved turning towards the door and then checking his watch.

'We just met two months ago,' he answers offhandedly.

'Yes, isn't it enough time to know a person?' she raises her eye brows.

'It's nothing like that,' he says.

Someone knocks on the door.

'Who is that?' Ved gets up suddenly.

Charu remains silent, looking at Ved and then at the door.

'*What if it's Angira*?' Ved thinks, noting how irresponsibly Charu made him stay longer than he intended.

'Don't worry, your surprise is still a surprise. Let me check who's at the door,' Charu gets up and opens the door.

Luck always favours those whose efforts and intentions are true, strong and pure. The person who knocked on the door is the guard who delivers letters for Angira. Ved smiles in relief when Charu announces that Angira will be delayed and won't be home till 8 p.m. It's 7.30 p.m. and he does not want to push his luck any more. In the next few hours, Angira will experience the magic of the surprise Ved has in store for her. On his way back home, he texts Charu an elaborate set of instructions on how to hand over the envelopes to Angira and hopes that Angira accepts the surprise in a desirable manner.

Ved and His Surprising Ways

Angira is sleepy as the clock inches towards her birthday. She is, however, still texting Ved while rolling on her bed, eventually falling asleep. At 11.30 p.m. when her phone begins ringing with calls from friends intending to wish her, she pulls it out from under her pillow. Along with the phone she pulls out an envelope as well.

'Charu, who kept this under my pillow?'

Charu is sleeping in her room. Having not received a reply, Angira answers the call before it gets disconnected. She walks in to find Charu sleeping like a log and covers her with a blanket. She continues taking calls from her friends from Delhi. By 11.59 p.m. Ved calls her. It's always a different feeling to be the first one to wish someone special at sharp 12 a.m.

'Wish you a very happy birthday,' he says immediately.

'Thank you so much,' Angira says.

She is happy that more than twenty people have called her before her birthday even began. She didn't think so many people would remember her birthday but they do.

'I just called to wish you. I am sure your family and friends must be calling you now. Enjoy your special day. Good night,' Ved wishes her.

She sits on the sofa while talking to Anushka and then Arjun. With her phone between her shoulder and ear, she tears the envelope. It has a card with a note written with a sparkle pen. Without reading its contents, she turns the card to check who has sent it to her. However, the card bears no name. For a moment, Angira recalls her past when she used to make these heart-shaped cards. She turns the card back and opens it. At that moment, someone knocks on the door. She leaves the card on the dining table.

Who could it be at this hour of the night? She reaches for the door and looks through the peephole. Her friends Neha and Rashi from college are standing outside with polybags. As soon as Angira opens the door, they shout birthday wishes to her. They walk straight into the apartment and into Charu's room.

'Hello, sexy Charu! Today is your babe's birthday and you are fucking sleeping,' Neha says and gives Angira a high five.

'What are you wearing, Neha? You look smoking hot,' Charu replies, now awake.

Neha is wearing a dress which perfectly fits her small waist and toned upper body. Rashi is also looking fabulous in a two-piece dress with nail art on her long nails, shiny lipgloss on her broad lips and fish-shaped earrings with small diamonds on it. When she smiles, she wins many hearts in an instant.

'Yes, all this is for the party tonight,' Neha winks and points to the bottle of vodka in the polybag she is holding.

'What is that?' Charu asks.

'A birthday gift for Angira,' she responds with naughty eyes.

Everyone settles down on the sofa and Neha places an unwrapped box on the table.

'Thank you guys, so, so much for coming. I was thinking of going home yesterday because I have never been alone on my birthday, but you guys made it perfect,' Angira looks happily at them.

She didn't expect this. Few minutes ago, the place was quiet and now it's noisy and it is going to get even noisier as the night progresses. Charu goes on to prepare everything for Angira's birthday. It just takes a few minutes to make sure everyone is in a party mood. Charu connects her phone to the woofer. She switches off the lights and puts on the LED disco bulb, which she and Angira had installed the day they moved into the apartment. The disco lights, not too jazzy and not too low, add just the right amount of understated elegance to the hall decor. Charu lights some candles around giving the room a romantic touch. With light music playing in the back, the ambience is just perfect.

'How's this? I bought it the day I was leaving for Delhi,' Neha asks Charu, showing off her dress.

'It's perfect. You are looking good. Anyway, even if you wore something else, you would still look great. The dress matters very little given how amazing you look,' Charu replies with a smile.

'But I can't be like you. You are the prettiest girl I know, and you have a great heart and a killer smile,' Neha smiles at Charu.

'Thanks, Charu. It's been a long time since I have been to any party. Thanks a lot for inviting me secretly,' Rashi says looking at all of them.

'Thank you. Thank you,' Charu says, joyous and lively.

The last time they all went to Hard Rock Cafe was when one of their faculties got nominated for an international fashion show being held in London. It was just a nomination, but it was reason enough for the girls to demand a treat from the nominee.

'But you won't drink today because I can't take care of you,' Neha teases Rashi.

'Guys, I need your attention,' Neha claps in the air.

'Yes, yes, we are listening,' Charu and Rashi reply. Angira looks attentive.

Neha takes a cake out of a box, saying, 'I got this specially made for our birthday girl.'

Everyone's eyes are on the cake. It's a cake shaped like a penis.

'Oh my god,' Angira starts laughing uproariously.

Charu cannot contain herself.

'You made it?' Angira questions.

She takes the berry fallen from the cake and eats it.

'Yes, don't ask about what I went through while baking it. Mom kept on coming into the kitchen. Finally I had to explain what I was doing without showing it to her,' Neha says while taking out candles from her bag.

Neha has turned this birthday party into an adult party with a bachelorette cake.

'There's something more as well,' Neha warns them.

Charu says, 'Show, show, what's that?'

'Wait...'

'It's an adult candle that goes with the cake,' Neha takes a long and thick penis-shaped candle and pushes it gently on top of the cake.

Everyone is amused.

'Wait, wait, we have one for you as well,' Rashi takes another one out from Neha's bag.

Charu takes the candle and stares at it before waving it at Angira and asking, 'Do you like this?'

'As I can see you are enjoying it more than I ever will,' Angira says, throwing a piece of lemon at her.

'Oh yeah, I am,' Charu is about to take the candle in her mouth.

Neha stops her. 'Calm down, calm down. If you want a realistic dong, go get a real dong,' Neha takes the candle back from her hand.

'Can we all take a selfie with the cake and these candles?' Charu asks the girls.

'Yeah!'

'Aha!'

Once the picture is clicked, Charu gets up. 'Let me get some matchsticks to light these candles.'

'Sit, sit. I have a lighter,' Neha takes out a lighter from her handbag.

'You have everything in your bag,' Angira says with a smile.

They are celebrating the moment by cutting the cake in the hall. Though the amusing cake and candles have taken most of her attention, Angira keeps looking at the card she left on the table. She wants to hide it somewhere. She is pretty sure that Charu must know about the envelope.

Everyone claps and now the party has officially begun.

'One.'

'Two.'

'Three!'

Angira cuts the cake and everyone wishes her once again.

'This is for you, Charu,' Angira takes the head of the penis and puts it into her mouth. Charu eats half of it and smears the rest on Angira's face.

Neha and Rashi follow suit, 'Wish you a very, very happy birthday. Keep smiling. We are blessed to have a friend like you. Love you, babe.'

Angira's neck and shoulders are smeared with cake. These childish moments are cherished by them all considering how hectic adult life can get in Mumbai. Once the initial birthday rituals are completed,

Angira asks Charu to accompany her to the kitchen.

'Hey Charu, sweetie come to the kitchen. I need your help.'

'Should I come as well?' Rashi asks and is about to get up.

'No, no, you sit, I'll just come. She can't survive without me. I wish she wouldn't need my help all the time,' Charu laughs and gets up to go to the kitchen.

'Who kept this under my pillow?' Angira asks her in a low voice.

'Oh yes, I was about to inform you. I got this in a courier this evening from the security guard. And there is a letter in your drawer as well.'

'Do you know where this letter came from?' Angira enquires.

'No. Someone may have sent it to you to give you a surprise. Chill! Let's go,' Charu says.

She takes four glasses and a plate of salted peanuts, and goes to the hall.

Angira finally reads the card. It says:

Everything has a reason, I do believe this.
But meeting you without any reason
has given me all the reasons to be with you.
Wish you a very happy birthday.

Angira knows who has written this card. There can be no other person except Ved. She wants to call him and express her gratitude for this kind gesture but everyone is waiting for her, so she writes to him on WhatsApp.

Thanks for the card and wishes,
So sweet of you.

You are welcome.
Enjoy your birthday.

'Hey, keep the phone aside,' Neha snatches Angira's phone and puts it away. Neha pours vodka and strawberry juice in an equal ratio in all four glasses, and a little more in her and Charu's glass.

'Hey, I won't have the drink. I'll just have orange juice,' Angira says, showing her displeasure at the sight of vodka.

'It is just vodka with strawberry juice, you can have it. It's your birthday, take this,' Neha offers her a glass.

She takes the glass and waits for the others to say cheers.

'Cheers to Angira!' Charu shouts, raising her glass.

'Cheers!'

'Cheers!'

'Cheers!'

They sit comfortably on the floor having finished a few rounds of drinks within fifteen minutes.

Charu smiles looking at everyone and nods, saying, 'Now may we all request Angira to come on the dance floor because the party tonight demands that she dance for us.'

They all dance and party hard until they are tired. Then they sleep wherever they get a place in the hall.

◊

A cold chill runs through Angira's calves as they all sleep on the sofa, while Charu passes out on the floor. The apartment is messy thanks to the party the night before. There is a knock on the door and Angira wakes up terrified, knowing that having late night parties in their building is not allowed. Thankfully, it is the garbage collector at the door. Once she has given him the garbage, she goes back into the hall.

'Charu, get up,' Angira pushes her a bit.

Angira sits on the chair and drinks water from a bottle which is on the dining table. She is hungover. She takes a few more sips. She replies to the birthday messages she received last night. Once she has dragged everyone to the bedrooms and put them off to sleep, she cleans the apartment. When the chores have been taken care of, she goes to the bathroom only to find a card next to her toothbrush. She easily guesses that it is the second card from Ved.

It says:

Sometimes, I act indifferently to get your attention,
You take all my worries and pain away, and fill my days with joy.
I feel good taking suggestions from you not because

I can't make decisions alone but because,
you complete me.
I hope you had a great night and birthday.

She washes her face and walks to the hall after reading the card again. She walks to her room and looks around on her bed for another card. The search is futile. She wanders to the kitchen hoping to make coffee for her friends, knowing it will help with the hangover. It is under the coffee jar that she finds another card. She excitedly opens it.

When I am about to say something,
You reach out to me at that very moment.
It has happened several times in the last sixty-seven days,
twenty-two hours and thirty minutes,
and it's not magic.
It's because we're on the same wavelength.
P.S. Now don't validate the time ;) It's an approximation.

She goes back to her room and starts checking everything, leaving the coffee jar and the pan on the stove unattended. She checks everything, from her handbag to the cupboard. It is then that she finds one more envelope in her handbag.

Gosh! How many are there? She doesn't read the card but goes on checking the whole room and then the hall. She wants to find every card before the others wake up, but she doesn't find any more. She reads the one she got:

I am not being cheesy, but it's hard to sleep without listening
to your voice.
It doesn't matter if I try to fight against my will, because I
still find all the reasons
To call you in the middle of the night just to listen to you.

Now Angira is feeling nostalgic about the moments they shared just in sixty-seven or sixty-eight days. She is in seventh heaven, and feels so happy and pampered with these cards with lovely messages written in them. Ved can be so creative. She never expected this of him given his busy schedule. However, he made it all possible. She smiles. She suddenly remembers that Charu said yesterday that there was a letter which came with these cards and it's in her drawer. She goes to her room and finds the letter but last line says:

> Please throw the other paper just to keep the surprise a surprise. Please :)

Angira feels like waking Charu up and asking her for the other letter, but she is still sleeping. Angira checks the dustbin and then realizes that she has given it to the garbage collector.

'Shit! Now what do I do?'

Angira is super charged to find all the cards. She runs to the hall and pokes her head out to check if she can spot the garbage collector downstairs.

⁂

Oh, this is madness! Are there any more? she wonders.

Arjun's words, about a bad past having little relevance in her happy future, come back to her. She smiles knowing Ved is around her and has become her best friend. She calls him to enquire about the fifth card.

'Thank you so much! You actually gave me goosebumps. But I hope you're not in love with me,' Angira thanks him and cracks a joke.

'Oh, is it? I just tried to make your birthday special and I am happy. Hope you're not missing home much now.'

'Yes, you did it. You deserve ten on ten for the effort.'

'So you got all the cards?' Ved asks nonchalantly, trying to find out if she has gotten all the cards or not.

He planned everything meticulously and hopes Charu can manage to help him execute his creative plan exactly the way he envisioned it.

'Yes, I got four cards,' Angira says, having kept all four of them in an envelope.

'You got only four?' he asks.

He wants her to read the fifth and last card which he considers to be the most special.

'Where is the fifth one?' she asks.

'It's there on the bed but at the foot of the bed.'

'Why did you keep it there?' Angira asks, shaking her head in disbelief.

'Because by the time you wake up in the morning, your head is near the foot of the bed,' he laughs.

'Smart...' Angira says over the call while turning the bed sheet and pulling up the corners of the mattress. Ved knows her so well and talking to her for long hours has helped him plan the surprise well.

'I checked everywhere on the bed, it's nowhere,' she checks her room one more time but she doesn't find it.

'Okay, leave it. I must have forgotten to give the last one,' Ved says, still wondering if he forgot to give the card to Charu.

'There are only four,' he lies knowing he will have to tell Angira about the fifth card if she does not find it. It will entail Ved confessing his love for her over the telephone, something he hopes to avoid.

'Ved, thank you so much! But you need to promise me something.'

'What?'

'You are the one I trust the most now. You helped me in every way. Never leave me and be my best friend forever,' she sounds poignant and emotional.

'I am always there for you. You just need to stop criticizing me when I play badly on the ground,' he laughs and tries to make her smile so she does not get too emotional since she is missing home.

Sometimes things don't go as planned. Ved wanted to propose to her today in his way and things turned upside down. However, Ved has not panicked. Maybe today was not the day. He knows there is always a tomorrow awaiting him. More importantly, he is happy to have her in his life.

The Final Card

It's been more than a week and Ved has not heard from Angira about the fifth card. Either the card was not in the envelope that was given to Charu or Charu must have misplaced it. Sitting alone at home, he thinks about Angira. He is hoping to meet her in the evening. Suddenly, his cellphone vibrates. It's Angira on WhatsApp.

Hey, what's up?

Hey! Hi.

He wonders if she has received the card but decides not to ask her about it. He thinks for a moment. *How can I be so silly? If I love her I should tell her. Why the hell am I playing this game?*

What's up?

Just came back from jogging,
Just relaxing on this lazy Saturday morning.
What about you?

Nothing, I am getting bored.
Charu has some project.
So she is in Delhi for two weeks.
I want to go too :(

Oh! That's sad.
No worries, enjoy your time.
Go shopping ;)

What are you doing?
Come home if you have time in the evening.

Ved pauses to think.

Are you inviting me?

No, I am getting bored so need your company.
I suggest you use your brains on the football pitch and not here.

Okay, okay. At what time?

Let's have dinner together.
I will cook something.

Oh my god! A Delhi Punjabi girl knows cooking.
Am I dreaming? Someone pinch me.

Ved, I know how to cook, okay.
Moreover, I have gotten better at cooking after coming to Mumbai.
I'll let you know when to leave.

Sure.

See you.
Need to finish some work.

Ved and Angira have always met each other for dinners and outings in the city. However, this is the first time they will meet at her apartment. He wants to make the night special and sees this as an opportunity to express his love for her. He starts getting ready and once he is in front of his cupboard, his hands automatically go to the white shirt he feels is lucky for him. After trying different combinations of outfits, Ved goes for his old favourite combination—blue and white. Ved reaches her place by 8 p.m.

∞

'Hello Mr Ved Gulati, welcome home,' Angira lets him in.

Ved sits on the sofa in the hall.

'What happened? What are you thinking?' she asks, wiping her face. She is looking fresh.

'Nothing, just a little thirsty,' he says in an effort to hide his nervousness.

She gets a water bottle for him from the kitchen. He utilizes the time to check himself on the screen of his phone.

Angira gives him the bottle and asks, 'You want to freshen up?'

Ved looks tired. He gulps down more than half of the bottle in one go. Angira smiles inside thinking all athletes are the same— fast but not furious, and forever energetic.

'Yeah, where is the washroom? I'll wash my face. It's humid outside,' Ved asks her while getting up and then looking outside from the window.

He can see children playing and the elderly walking in the garden. Angira shows him the way to the washroom. After Ved washes his face, he comes out of the washroom.

'Do you want a towel?' she asks him, going in her room.

'No, I have a handkerchief,' he responds, wiping his face with the small piece of cloth.

Ved goes to the extreme corner of the apartment near the window and looks outside, by which time Angira comes into the hall, holding a card in her hand. Before Ved is able to recognize it Angira shows him the card and asks, 'Was this the last card, Ved?'

They both are standing at the extreme corners of the room. Ved doesn't respond to her. He didn't expect this to happen. He pauses to think. There is such a sense of uncertainty in the air. He nods without saying anything. In this moment Angira looks gorgeous, more beautiful than ever.

'You could have told me this. Were you scared?' There is a sense of uncontainable happiness on her face.

'It's never too late. I can say it now,' Ved smiles and continues, 'I love you, not just because you are beautiful but because you make me happy when I am with you.'

She just smiles listening to him, standing in the corner. She hasn't moved a step closer to him. Ved takes the initiative. He walks to her. She looks calm, but there is an uncertainty in her eyes. Ved breathes in her scent and takes her soft hand in his own.

'What happened?' she asks.

'Nothing, I like looking at you...' he smiles.

He touches her lips with his thumb and then her lips start quivering. He comes closer and can feel the warmth of her breath on his lips. He kisses her softly. There is no hesitation between them. Love takes its own course. No planning ever works in this sphere. Knowing this, he holds her tightly in his arms. Neither of them wants this moment to end. Fearing that if they blink the moment will end, they hold on to each other.

'I love you too,' Angira says looking into his eyes.

'I didn't say yet...' Ved gazes at her.

'Well, you already said those words to me last week in this card,' she grins, showing him the card.

'I love you,' he says kissing her hands.

'C'mon let's have some food, you must be hungry,' Angira releases him from her grip.

'I am not hungry,' he refuses to release her.

'You didn't eat anything. Let's eat something. I cooked for you,' she pushes him softly.

'Just two minutes, I am feeling good.'

They hug each other a little more firmly this time.

'Then never leave me,' she kisses him on his chest.

They are standing in the hall and the moon outside seems closer than before.

'You'll have other days to do all this. Let's have dinner first. You must be hungry, Ved,' she says.

He sits on the chair and finds the envelopes with all the cards. He places the last one along with the others, while Angira serves food for both of them.

'You are such a romantic. I never thought you'd be but I wish this goes on till our last breath,' she pours water in his glass.

'I am much more than you think,' he says with a smile, putting a chapati on his plate.

'As long as I give you some more leverage,' Angira says, patting him on his shoulder.

Happy Hours

'Can't you stay here tonight?' Angira asks Ved while getting up from the chair.

She wants him to be with her tonight. These moments are rare and don't come by always.

'Are you sure?' he asks while washing his hand in the basin.

'Yes. Charu will come after two weeks,' she repeats herself.

'I am asking if I can stay here. Are you sure about it?' He wipes his hands.

'What's wrong in that?' Angira asks, taking all the vessels to the kitchen.

'There is nothing wrong,' Ved answers

He walks in the hall randomly as he does every day after dinner. He remembers that he has to go with Arjun for an event tomorrow, but he doesn't want to go away from her either.

'*What should I do*?' he wonders.

'Then stay here,' Angira insists.

'Okay,' Ved checks his cellphone standing near the window.

He messages Arjun that he will stay at a friend's place tonight and will reach home on time tomorrow.

'What are you doing?' she asks, standing far away from him.

'Just dropping a message to Arjun. Otherwise, he is going to kill me if I don't reach home on time. Tomorrow he has an event. I have to go with him for it.'

'What? What name did you just say?' Angira asks.

'Arjun. Why, what happened? He called you or what?' he turns his back on the couple walking in the park holding hands.

'Arjun, the author?' she asks him again.

'You have read his books? You know him?' Ved asks her, sitting on the sofa.

'Fuck.' Angira can't believe that Ved knows Arjun. 'How do you know him?' She is totally confused and surprised.

'What happened? We are flatmates,' he doesn't understand what's going on in her mind.

'Nothing. Can you give me your phone? I want to see his picture,' Angira sits next to him and takes his phone.

'But what happened?' Ved doesn't know what's going on.

'Nothing,' Angira gets his phone.

Ved takes his phone back and shows her the WhatsApp picture of Arjun. She is amazed and shocked. She is just stunned as she tries to connect everything that has happened.

'He is Anushka's best friend. I know everything about him. He is the one who convinced my mom to let me come to Mumbai to study fashion designing,' Angira informs Ved. 'Does he know about us?' she asks him.

'No, he doesn't. This is going to be a little awkward,' Ved has mixed feelings.

Angira tries to connect everything but fails to understand how Ved and Arjun can be flatmates in the most crowded city. Ved is also surprised. The world is indeed small. At the same time, to have something like this happen in Mumbai is unheard of.

'But I am still confused. How do you know each other?' she asks.

'We are from the same college,' says Ved.

'Really?' she asks again.

'Yes. Anushka, Arjun and I were classmates of Jaypee University,' Ved explains everything about their friendship and the moments they spent together during their college days.

'Seriously, this is unexpected,' she feels like everything has an underlying intention.

'So you getting my number was not a coincidence? Did Anushka give you my number?' he enquires.

'No, I haven't even discussed about you with Anushka,' she says and recalls that on the night they went to the karaoke bar, she used Arjun's phone to call Anushka and then saved his number on her phone. What happened later at the girl's hostel has somehow been a hazy memory.

'The unexpected is always meant to happen,' says Ved and kisses Angira on her hand. 'I love you.'

'But this is beyond my expectations. You know what happened yesterday? We were on a conference call and Anushka was asking Mom what if Arjun liked me,' Angira says while holding his palms in her own.

Ved doesn't say anything.

'What do you think?' he asks her.

'He is a nice guy. I like him and I respect him more than anyone, but I love you more than anything else. So don't be possessive,' she smiles looking at him.

Does Arjun have feelings for Angira? He never told me about Angira. Maybe Anushka and Arjun like each other.

'Should I tell Arjun about us?' Ved asks Angira.

'No, don't tell him about us as of now. Else he'll tell Anushka and then my mom will call me back to Delhi for sure.'

'Don't worry.'

He starts kissing Angira on the sofa. She responds softly. Soon it gets intense.

'It feels so good to be with you,' he says softly into her ears. 'Let's go into the room.'

'No,' she says.

Things are moving smoothly; she places her head on his shoulder and he touches her earrings, planting a soft kiss on her neck. They both are lying on the sofa. Angira is looking at the ceiling.

Ved glances at her and he puts his index finger on her lips, 'I love you, and I just want to love you forever. Don't leave me ever.'

'I love you too.'

Holding her even more firmly, he softly kisses her on her forehead.

'What are you doing?' she asks.

'I just don't want to leave you.'

She runs her fingers through his hair.

'Let's go to the bedroom,' she says tenderly.

Within moments they end up in the bedroom.

'You want a water bottle?' she asks him.

'Yes.'

The moment Angira comes back, Ved grabs her by the waist as she's switching off the lights. Lying in bed, they cuddle gently.

'Is this our Happy Hours?' Angira asks, still playing with his hair.

'Yes, it is. Don't you think so?'

'I like your hair,' she runs her hand through his hair.

'Remove this,' Ved pulls her shirt.

'No,' she responds and holds his hand.

'Please, I want to kiss you again,' he pulls her t-shirt off, and taking off his own, throws them somewhere in the room.

'Why do you wear a bra at night?' he asks.

'Usually I don't but...' she is just about to finish her sentence when Ved unhooks her bra and throws it away.

They are almost naked.

'You're too fast. How many girls have you slept with?'

'Shut up! I never think of the past. It was a nightmare,' Ved looks a little serious, but as soon as Angira kisses him he forgets all his troubles.

She doesn't want to discuss the past either. She just wants to cherish these moments and share them with Ved.

'But you look hot and attractive. Girls must surely check you out,' she asks him again.

'Do you think so? I have never turned up for any girl yet. You could be the special one. Now don't distract me. I am not going to leave you.'

He starts kissing her neck.

She laughs and moves his hand away, 'Ved, stop, I feel ticklish.'

But Ved continues...

Angira moans and grabs his shoulders. He gently puts his palms on her breasts and squeezes them.

'Stop it, Ved. It's hurting...I am not well,' she says.

Ved moves his hands over her pants, and says, 'I want to take this off.'

'Not now...please!'

He slides his fingers into her pants.

'Stop it, please, don't do that.'

'Yes.'

'No.'

'Please,' she turns away. She seems nervous and looks like she is thinking of something else.

'Why?' Ved doesn't want to leave her.

'I may have my period. It may happen anytime. I am sorry,' she looks embarrassed and apologetic.

'Hey, don't be sorry. I love you. Are you in pain?' Ved understands.

'Yes, my stomach is aching.'

'I am so sorry, I didn't know,' Ved looks embarrassed.

'Just chill, I am not sick. It just happens before chums. Hope you don't mind seeing me like this,' she smiles.

'I know you are not sick, but I am concerned. I know it happens with a lot of women.'

'Ahem, you know a lot,' Angira looks at him. 'Don't worry. I will put a hot waterbag on my stomach and the pain will be gone,' Angira says while putting on her clothes.

'No, you sit. I'll get it for you,' Ved says while wearing his clothes.

'Chill, I'll get it for myself,' she pulls him back on the bed.

'Shut up. You lie down, I'll get it. Just instruct me how to get through the mess in your house,' he gives her a pillow and follows her instructions.

He goes to the kitchen to warm some water. He comes back with a hot waterbag and a water bottle. A towel hangs on his shoulder.

'You wet my bedsheet,' Angira says.

'I'll change it,' Ved says, feeling embarrassed.

I should have worn a condom.

'What are you thinking? Hey chill, that's okay' she says, teasing him.

'Wait, I'll change it,' he pulls the bedsheet off.

'That's okay, Ved. I'll do that.'

'Will you please lie down for some time?'

Angira lies on the bed. Ved takes the hot waterbag and then keeps it on her stomach. He looks over her till she sleeps off and covers her with a bedsheet, then checks her cupboard to get a pad for her. He searches the whole room but doesn't find any. He risks breaking the protocol of a girl's privacy and goes to Charu's room. He opens her cupboard and takes the packet and keeps it on the table near her bed. He goes to the hall and watches some television shows.

In a while, he too falls asleep after setting an alarm to go with Arjun to his event early next morning.

Happiness Is Sharing Secrets

The month of October arrives. Angira is spending a lazy Saturday night chatting with her friend from Delhi. Suddenly, Iona writes to her on Facebook. Though they hit it off quite well on the only night they had spent together in Delhi, they had sparingly kept in touch due to their conflicting schedules. She writes back to Iona, 'Hey Iona, send me your number.'

Iona responds promptly. Angira calls her.

'Hey! How are you?' Iona says over the call.

She seems excited to hear from Angira. Angira hopes that Iona can come to Mumbai soon, something she had promised a long time ago.

'I am good. You just forgot me. You are so mean,' Iona puts the blames on Angira.

'No, I still remember you,' Angira replies playfully, poking fun at her. 'I actually messaged you on the number I had saved that night. Turned out to be a wrong number thanks to us being completely buzzed at that unforgettable party. It's like I can only remember a few scenes from that night and the rest have vanished like those smoke rings.'

'Yeah, you were quite drunk that day. But that was an amazing night out! We were talking nonsense. Anyway, I have good news,' Iona says eagerly.

'Are you pregnant?' Angira laughs again.

'Shut up,' Iona says lovingly. 'I am coming to Mumbai for garba night next month.'

'That's great! Awesome news,' Angira says excitedly. 'I am missing you guys. I am bored here. Anushka is also coming next month. When are you coming exactly?' she confirms the date because she thinks of inviting everyone to come to Mumbai around the same time.

'I'll be there on the first week of the next month.'

'Oh.'

'What happened,' Iona questions.

'Nothing, I'll tell Anushka to come a week before. Then we can go for garba night together. Or the two of you can coordinate and reach Mumbai at the same time,' Angira says, counting the days on her fingers.

'Yes, that's a good idea actually,' Iona confirms her dates and makes a mental note to call Anushka after talking to Angira.

I'm going to make that week unforgettable. I have heard so much about the garba night here. Angira plans it out in her mind.

'Okay, done. So what else is happening? How's life in Mumbai?' Iona asks.

Girls have so many things to talk, but Angira doesn't know where to start.

'Life is good. I met someone here,' Angira says and before she can elaborate, Iona interrupts her.

'Are you serious?'

'Yeah, will tell you when you get here.'

'You got lucky just on reaching Mumbai. I'm happy for you. Keep smiling sweetie,' Iona laughs. 'So, did you kiss him?' she asks candidly.

Times have changed—people exchange kisses before exchanging proposals.

'I'll tell you everything once you come here,' Angira wants to keep it a surprise for everyone. Iona uses her sense and tries to guess what must have happened between them. Angira doesn't want to tell anybody about Ved because of a few reasons. She doesn't want Anushka and her mom to find out because they will call her back to Delhi. Whatever hurt her in the past was because of a guy, so she wants to remain cautious. It's difficult to convince Indian families about a love marriage. Though Punjabi families tend to be liberal, her family is against the concept of a love marriage, just like Arjun's.

'So what's his name, what does he do? At least tell me something. Now I am excited to know your story,' Iona says, feeling happy for Angira.

A month ago, Angira wasn't even ready to believe in any kind of relationship and now she talks positively about love and relationships.

She is enjoying her life.

'His name is Ved Gulati and he is a football player,' Angira says, describing how her relationship started in the first place.

'And where does he live? Is he in Mumbai?' Iona asks.

'Yes. Soon, he is going to play for a Kolkata team as well. He is such a nice guy. Actually, we kissed last week. My roommate was out, so I called him for dinner and then unexpectedly things happened.'

'Oh my god! You are such a fast ass. Did anything else happen?' Iona teases her.

'Nothing. I love him. He is such a sweet guy,' Angira says and then realizes that she ended up revealing everything.

'So what, if you love him you won't have sex with him? Have you told Anushka about him?' Iona says.

'No, only Charu knows and now you. You and Anushka come to Mumbai, let's meet up and then I'll tell everyone. Please don't tell anybody right now. I need to plan how to disclose this news the right way.'

'Good idea. Sure, I won't.'

The new generation is growing and getting smarter at a faster rate. Now we have started talking about relationships openly with our families, which has helped resolved so many issues. Things will get even better once we can talk about sex openly without being judged.

So It's Just You and Me Now

It's been more than a week since Ved and Angira last met. Angira has been busy with her work, while Ved is getting bored sitting alone at home. He decides to call her to his apartment to spend time with her.

'Are you sure? Have you told Arjun about us?' she asks him.

'He isn't home,' Ved replies.

'Are you sure he won't be home anytime soon?' Angira asks one more time.

'He will be back early morning on Monday,' Ved confirms. 'At what time will you leave?'

'Can we meet in the evening? I need to wrap up some work with Charu,' she says.

Charu shouts at the back, 'Ved, please take care of her. Keep her in your control. She troubles me a lot these days!'

'Just ignore Charu. She has gone mad,' Angira says playfully.

'Are you going to stay with me tonight?' he asks her, planning to cook for her in case she stays over. Ved wants to take the opportunity to show off his cooking skills.

'Are you inviting me, Mr Gulati?'

'What do you want me to say?'

'Invite me nicely,' she laughs.

'Angira. I'm going to kick your ass. Get up, breakfast is ready,' Charu shouts from the hall.

'Need to go. I'll text you once I leave. And listen, I love you,' she kisses him over the call.

'Wait, what's your favourite dish? I want to cook for you today,' he asks her excitedly.

'Are you joking?'

'I am not a great cook but good enough to be able to feed you well for a lifetime as your life partner,' he says.

'These are false promises. Nobody does all this after the wedding,'

Angira tells him the truth about Indian husbands.

'I will. I promise. You just need to stand by my side,' he assures her and this means a lot to Angira.

'Wow. You know all the tricks to impress a girl. Don't be cheesy,' she gets up as Charu has served her omelette for breakfast.

'Okay, forget that. Now tell me what's your favourite dish?' he asks her again.

'Cook anything you feel like. Let me see what you can come up with. By the way, I am totally impressed by you. Now let me go. Bye.'

❧

Ved cleans the whole house. Arjun is surely going to be shocked to see that he did everything on his own. Once he is done with his household duties, he calls Angira.

'Where are you, Angira,' he asks over the call.

'I am on the way. It will take some time to reach there,' Angira replies, her voice barely audible from a crowded bus.

'Are you in a bus?' Ved asks.

'Yeah.'

'Is it crowded?' he is excited to see her but is also very concerned about her.

'Ved, I am perfectly fine,' she says. Coming close to the microphone, she murmurs, 'We both want to meet, so someone has to take an initiative. This time I am taking it and I happen to be travelling in a crowded bus.'

Angira is not comfortable in the local trains and buses of Mumbai. She only enjoys them when she travels to meet Ved. To alleviate her pain, Ved cracks jokes while she travels.

'Where have you reached?' he asks.

'Ved, this is the sixth time you are asking this question in the last thirty-five minutes. Give me fifteen to twenty minutes, I'll be there,' Angira says, shrugging her shoulder. 'Okay bye,' she disconnects the call.

'Bye. Take care.'

Now Ved gets time to cook. He keeps the bottle in the freezer thinking that Angira will be thirsty after the commute to his place. He rushes and finishes cooking everything by the time Angira rings the doorbell. If Ved was not a footballer, he would have surely been a chef.

He decides to cook something special for her. In a bowl, he mixes maida and baking powder. He removes the chocolate from the pan once it has melted and pours it into that mixture. He has placed his watch on the slab near the oven and he keeps checking it while beating the mixture. Buttering the baking pan, he then fills it with the mixture. After putting it in the oven, he sets the time and temperature. He wants to impress Angira one more time with a skill that every Indian girl looks for in a guy these days.

∞

'Pudhe chala! pudhe chala!' the bus conductor shouts. These are the first words Angira had heard when she stepped foot in Mumbai. She was new to the city then, so it took a few days and some scolding from the bus conductors to know the meaning of pudhe chala, which means 'move ahead'.

She understands the city a lot better now. The city makes her happy. These thoughts flood her mind as she finds herself standing outside Ved's home. She rings the doorbell.

'Hello,' she says as Ved opens the door.

'Come,' Ved greets her with a hug.

'So, what's up?'

'Nothing. I was just waiting for you,' Ved says with a smile.

He makes her sit on the sofa and gives her a glass of nimbu pani.

'Do you like nimbu pani?' she asks.

'No, but it provides instant energy,' he says.

Angira starts laughing, 'Okay. Thanks.'

'Why are you laughing? It's true,' he seems exasperated.

'No, nothing. You are a mad fellow.'

'Okay, you must be tired. You can use the face wash there,' he shows her the way to the washroom.

Angira doesn't take much time and when she reaches the hall, Ved pulls the curtains aside. There's a mat on the floor of the balcony, with a bottle of wine and two glasses. It's 7.30 p.m. It's a little dark outside but they can see each other.

'Isn't this a little too romantic, Ved?'

Angira sits in the balcony, resting her chin on her knees and wrapping her hands around her legs. She looks a little serious.

'Don't you like romance?' Ved says, lighting few candles in the hall and two in the balcony.

With a candlelit balcony, soft sensual music playing in the hall and a bottle of red wine, this evening looks so romantic.

'No, I can't believe that you are this romantic.'

Ved comes and sits right next to her.

'Don't make that face,' he looks at her and grins.

He pours wine in the glasses and gives one to her.

'Okay. Thanks,' she smiles and takes the glass.

'You know what? Whenever I feel lonely or sad, I come here and sit in the balcony. It brings me peace. I wanted to share that with you, that's why I set this up in the balcony. I am going to cherish this moment forever,' he says.

'You breathe romance, Ved. I am not at all romantic,' she clinks the glass and they both drink the wine.

'Just give me a minute,' Ved says, going to the hall.

Turning back to Angira, he says, 'Now, Ved Gulati is presenting the most sensational part of the evening to you.'

He brings out a plate full of chocolate brownies he made before she arrived.

'Oh my god...you made this?' Angira puts aside her glass and takes the plate delightfully.

Ved nods, 'For you.'

'Oh my god,' Angira moves to make some space for the plate.

'Sit, sit, I can manage.'

'You really made this for me?' Angira is still surprised. Ved nods and then smiles, 'Yup.'

They sit and have an intimate conversation. Sometimes you don't need physical touch to be intimate; your words can make moments far more intimate than your acts. They both enjoy a memorable time with a glass of wine and the chocolate brownies on this romantic evening. They don't realize when the time passes.

Angira is looking at those candles that Ved lit an hour ago. The candles have become small but are still able to spread some light in the balcony. She is looking at them when a sudden gust of cold breeze blows them out. It is suddenly dark.

Ved holds Angira in his arms and they kiss passionately. This becomes an unforgettable night for them—one that Ved will never find the words to describe.

The Anglo-Indian

Having spent considerable time together, Ved wants to tell Angira the truth about his family. He feels she will understand his situation. But there is a part of him that wonders if she will be able to face the truth, despite her love for him. He wants to tell her everything before long, so he can take their relationship forward.

Holding a glass of water in one hand, he slides the window of his room completely to the left and lets the cool breeze in. The streets outside are empty. The fragrance of honeysuckle makes its way in. Birds have stopped twittering.

I don't want to hide anything. He decides to tell her everything.

He finds Angira's eyelash on his cheek and decides to make a wish for both of them.

'Do you really believe in this? I did this almost every time I found an eyelash, but nothing happened. Maybe my wishes ask too much of the man above,' Angira grins at him.

Ved suddenly opens his eyes. Embarrassed, he shoves his hands into the pockets of his shorts pretending he was doing nothing, but it is too late. Angira has understood that there is something on his mind. They have been with each other for months and they understand each other without words.

'But if it worked, I would be the happiest person in the world,' she says, trying to make him smile.

He keeps looking outside and doesn't say a word.

'What happened to you, Ved? You don't look all right. I mean you aren't saying anything. If you want to talk about something, you should,' Angira holds his hand in hers and looks at him. 'Please don't put any tag of relationship, expectations and formalities. I believe we like each other's company. Let's live the rest of our lives the way we have lived till now.'

Ved wants to say something, but he is not able to find the courage to speak up. But he believes there is no point hiding the truth.

'You know, I love this place. I could live here forever. I could stand here all day, holding you in my arms and just looking outside,' Angira says, looking into his eyes, and kisses him on his cheeks before hugging him.

'Ved, I love you. I want to listen to you when you feel like sharing something,' she says and steps towards the room again.

'Angira, wait,' Ved turns and stops her.

She turns back and stands next to him. 'Yeah,' she says.

'Angira, you are the most important person in my life now. We have come to that point where we share everything with each other. So I have decided to tell you something that I have never told anybody, not even my close friends, except Arjun. I love you and I want to marry you, but would like to know if you want to marry me. I am an Anglo-Indian.'

'What does that mean?' she asks.

'I am not from your community. Our roots go back to the Anglo-Indian community. My grandmother was one of them. My grandfather, who was British, left her here when the East India Company left. She was brutally beaten, humiliated and insulted by the people in our society. She was treated like a prostitute. People used to say that my father was born in a brothel. Being a kid I couldn't shut them up. That's why when you asked that day about my family I avoided telling you all this.'

'Where is your family, Ved?' she is shocked to hear about his family and the life of Anglo-Indians.

'They are in Kolkata.'

Ved doesn't speak any more. It is obvious that he is feeling sentimental.

'Ved, you know what? When I saw you for the first time, I didn't ask you about your religion. I didn't ask you about your community or your background, where you live, what you do. I just believed in the words you wrote to me and your face, which said enough about you.'

'Will your family agree with us being together?'

'I love you, Ved.'

'That doesn't answer my question. Will your family agree to this marriage?' Creases appear on his forehead.

'Ved, we'll talk to our families,' Angira replies, not convinced herself because she knows how difficult it will be to make her family agree to this marriage.

'Will they agree? I have a mom and a sister. They're still exploited in the society. My elder sister is turning thirty-three and nobody is ready to marry her because we are fucking Anglo-Indians. Is it my fault that a British guy came and fucked my grandmother, and left us all like this? We are suffering for no fucking reason,' Ved looks frustrated and pissed off.

He was expecting a straight answer from Angira that she will marry him.

'Why don't you call your family to Mumbai?' Angira holds his hand and they sit on the sofa.

'I want to, but they think they will become a hurdle in my career. Now that I have a scholarship to study here, I will call them soon. You asked me that day why I am doing an MBA. The reason is that I don't want my family to suffer anymore,' Ved hopes that he'll make everything perfect one day.

Angira kisses him and holds him more tightly, 'I love you. Everything will be okay and this doesn't change anything between us.' She punches him on his bum and adds, 'I am always with you.'

'I hope you are,' Ved says and they hug each other for some time.

Now the biggest obstacle is not just to tell Anushka but to make her mom and dad accept Ved's presence in her life. Angira understands the first step is to inform Anushka about Ved.

'Listen! We are planning to go for garba night next week. Anushka is also coming from Delhi, so I want you to be there. Be ready,' Angira drags him to the sofa and they sit at ease.

'Okay. I hope she likes me,' Ved says, looking into her eyes.

'She is very selective but don't worry, I'll tell you ways to impress her,' she winks and adds, 'It's not that easy to marry this girl.'

'I know,' Ved says and adds, 'but she knows me from my college days and this is going to be a shock for her. I think I should tell Arjun before talking to Anushka, because they are best friends and they share a close relationship. And Arjun can help us in case Anushka thinks I am not right for you.' Ved laughs and plans everything like a secret agent.

'So how's your best friend, Arjun?' Angira asks Ved.

'He is fine. You know, there was a time when we used to do everything together, but after college he has become quite serious. I just moved in with him a few months ago, so it will take some time for us to get back to our old ways.'

'Chill. Now you are with me, so everything will go smoothly. Moreover, if something needs to be discussed, one of you has to take the initiative,' Angira pulls his chin and kisses him on his cheeks.

'Once he gets time off work, I am going to ask him if he has any problem with me. I moved in with him because Anushka told me to. If he has any issues then he should just tell me.'

'Chill, he is a nice guy. I know him. He must be busy with things. You know how he behaves when he is stuck with work. Is your phone vibrating?' Angira can feel a vibration.

'No,' Ved looks conscious and takes his cellphone out from his pocket.

Angira takes the cellphone from his hand to see who's calling. Ved takes the phone back from her hand.

'Give it to me for a minute,' Ved unlocks the phone and goes through the recent calls and WhatsApp. He quickly deletes a WhatsApp chat.

'What is so important that you're not giving me your phone? Are you deleting your WhatsApp chat?' Angira feels weird about the way Ved is being protective of his cellphone.

'It's nothing, okay take the phone. I was just deleting the junk,' Ved gives her his cellphone and take her into the room.

Those Pretty Gujju Girls, Followed by the Punjabans

'Someone is so busy these days, they are not even answering my calls,' Anushka tells Arjun over a call. Ved is around watching videos on YouTube on his cellphone.

'Nothing like that, just stuck with work for the last couple of days. You know very well how difficult it is for me to manage writing and the job. After all this there's hardly any time for me to sleep,' Arjun says on reaching home.

'How much do you want to earn, lad?' Anushka asks, poking fun at him.

Ved can easily guess that Anushka is on the call. Ved thinks of telling Arjun about Angira. He messages Angira instead.

Hey! Should I tell Arjun about us?

What do you think? Should we?

I don't know.

Or let's drop the bomb on garba night, what say?

I'd rather tell Anushka and not Arjun.
He is very busy. He doesn't even talk to me properly.
I'll call you later. I've got to go now.

Sure.

'Nothing like that. Don't worry, I'll come to Delhi soon,' Arjun feels relaxed when he talks to Anushka.

Anushka is the only friend who he talks to almost every day. However, lately he's been swamped at work. Arjun gets up from the hall and goes to the other room.

'Arjun, your wallet,' Ved calls him back.

Arjun turns back smiling as he takes the wallet. He gives Ved an envelope.

'I found this in the postbox downstairs,' Arjun hands over the envelope.

Ved takes it. Arjun goes to his room, talking to Anushka over the call. Ved remembers the days when Arjun would pretend to be his father, uncle or his elder brother when the registrar wanted to talk to his family members. Ved suddenly smiles. He opens the envelope and reads the letter. He takes time to react. Finally, Ved has received the letter inviting him for the selection process in Kolkata next week for the Kolkata football team. He has finally gotten the chance that he fought for day and night.

❧

'You need a soulmate now,' Anushka says. It's in her nature to make Arjun laugh.

You always need a friend who can make you laugh even when you are crying. One does not need a friend who always gives you gyan to do this and that. Arjun quite enjoys these moments with her.

'Actually, even I think the same. What about you? If you concentrate on dieting for a few days you might get one too!' Arjun teases her.

'Come and talk to Mom. If she says yes, then I'll think about it. By the way, in college you used to run after the chubby girls. "They give more pleasure," these were your words, right?' Anushka teases him.

'I was immature back then,' Arjun replies.

'No, no, I remember each and everything. Should I open the whole Gazette of Arjun,' Anushka adds. 'Now listen, are you free next week?'

'I am going to Pune on an official trip,' Arjun replies. 'Why, what happened? Are you coming to Mumbai or what?'

'Yes, I am coming next week.'

'Seriously?' Arjun is surprised by her sudden plan.

'Can't you take a sick leave next week?' Anushka starts giving him excuses he can use.

'No, no, this time I won't go with your plan. Last time you sisters took to me to that party and at the airport how I got through the security check only I know. I was completely drunk!'

'So we won't drink this time,' Anushka wants him to come.

'Sweetie, on a serious note. I have already told them. Also, I have never danced the garba. I don't even know how to hold those sticks,' Arjun says.

'We don't use sticks in garba, we use them in dandiya.'

'Yeah, same.'

Anushka laughs.

'You should know that I'll hate you for ditching me.'

'I am sorry. We'll meet once I come to Delhi. Promise! By the way, Ved can come if you need any help. I think he is going with someone,' Arjun says, coming out of the room.

'Of course he is coming with me. You are the one who won't be there,' Anushka is happy to come to Mumbai but if Arjun could join them, the event would be more memorable.

'He is here by the way, you can talk to him,' Arjun gives the phone to Ved saying, 'Anushka is on the call.'

'Hey Abby, what's up?'

Ved calls her Abby since college as her full name is Anushka Batra.

He shows the letter to Arjun while talking to her. Arjun reads it completely.

'You did it, dude!' Arjun exclaims.

'What happened?' Anushka asks Ved.

'Nothing, that was Arjun. By the way I have good news,' he says in an excited and joyous tone.

'So when are you going,' Arjun murmurs.

Ved points out the date on the letter and continues talking. Arjun gives a thumbs up.

'What's that?' Anushka asks.

'I have been called for the Kolkata football team. Though it's the selection process, I hope I'll hit the right notes,' Ved replies.

'That's awesome, champ! Now I need a big party, with you sponsoring some shots for me,' Anushka always has a plan.

'It is just a screening,' Ved tries to make her understand the process.

'I know, I know, but they didn't send me the letter, they sent it you, which means you deserve it. If you deserve that, then I deserve a party.'

Ved and Anushka talk over the phone for a while.

Day after tomorrow, Arjun will travel from Mumbai to Pune.

Taking the lift to the 4th floor, Angira and Charu reach Ved's place.

Ved, Angira and Charu are drunk because Charu wanted to get high before reaching the venue. They both gave her company. This allowed Ved and Angira to spend time with each other as well. By the end of the evening, Ved is so drunk he needs lemonade before he can get to the venue.

'I told you not to drink, but you guys...you don't listen,' Angira says, looking worried

Ved takes a sip of the lemonade.

'I am fine,' Ved says.

'He is fine,' Charu says, smiling.

'I am fine. By the time we leave, I'll be perfect,' Ved gets up.

'At what time will we be leaving?' Charu asks Ved.

'You guys get ready. We'll leave at 6.30 from here,' Ved says, checking his cellphone. 'Guys, few of my college friends are also joining.'

He looks at the mirror where he can see Angira getting ready.

'Nice. Charu may get lucky,' Angira remarks.

'Where is Anushka?' Ved enquires getting up from the bed.

'She is at our flat.' Angira is wearing a lehenga and big earrings. She is looking like a Gujarati girl. The red and green colour combination of the lehenga suits her.

'Charu, can you and Angira pick up Anushka and reach Kora Kendra. I'll pick up my friends and then see you all there,' Ved says as Charu is more familiar with these places than Ved.

'Ved, you are drunk. Tell them to come directly. You can't go in this state,' Angira turns to him and says authoritatively.

'Now, don't behave like an Indian girlfriend. I am fine,' Ved replies and then he realizes Angira may feel bad. 'Okay, I will take the car to Jignesh's house and then he'll drive. Cool? Now, see you guys at the venue.'

'Sure.'

Jignesh is his Gujarati classmate and he also wants to come for the garba dance.

'Okay, I'll get ready and leave,' he comes closer to Angira. 'Don't be nervous,' Ved softly pats her shoulder.

'Yeah, I am fine,' Angira says.

'See you there,' Ved kisses her on her cheek.

'Are you taking Arjun's car?' Angira asks him since she wanted to go with him in the car.

'Yes, at least I can take advantage of his absence.'

'Okay, cool. Call me if you reach before us.'

'Sure.'

He gets ready and leaves to pick up his friends and reaches the venue directly.

Everyone is all set to go. Angira and Charu reach their apartment to pick up Anushka. They then pick up Iona from her friend's home and take a cab together.

'See what I got for you,' Charu says, showing Iona a few bottles in the cab.

'Orange juice?' Iona says jokingly.

'Guys, don't do that. I am not responsible if anything happens,' Anushka warns Iona not to drink.

'Guys are cooler in Mumbai and Gujju guys are so innocent and shareef, they won't trouble us,' Charu answers as Iona breaks into laughter.

'I don't know about that, but be sure you remain in your senses,' while Anushka completes the sentence, Iona has finished a bottle in one go.

'So are you guys ready for the bright colours and rhythmic steps of garba?' Charu asks the group.

'Have we reached?' Iona and Anushka ask together.

'Just a few more minutes...'

Mumbai is infamous for its traffic, but they manage to reach the destination on time. Angira and Iona talk, and she tells her all about the famous landmarks in Mumbai. Everyone is excited to celebrate these nine nights of revelry in the city that never sleeps. Mumbai has a huge Gujarati population and the city celebrates this festival with great fervour.

People, especially ladies, in the crowd are already discussing what they wore last Navratri.

'Anushka, there is one problem,' Iona says.

'What happened?' Anushka comes closer to listen to her as they're in a crowd and she is not audible.

'We are short of passes. We need two more, right?' Iona asks.

'No, we need three passes. Ved and his friends are also coming,' Anushka says.

'Ved,' she looks at Angira.

'Three?' she asks, surprised, and tries to come up with a solution.

'We won't get them,' Charu tells Angira who is already requesting a person at the counter for passes but it seems they're sold out.

'They have passes,' Charu points to the counter where Angira is standing.

'Yes, but they won't give us. We have to buy them in black,' Iona says.

'What the fuck,' Anushka says in frustration.

Getting passes in events like these at the last moment means one has to pay three times more than the original price and it doesn't even guarantee one an entry. 'Is there any other way to get passes?' Anushka and the group are collectively thinking about how to get it.

'Do any of you know how to speak in Gujarati?' Charu asks the group and adds, 'Yeah, if you know Gujarati and look sexy, you may get the passes.'

Everyone looks at each other and bursts out laughing.

'Okay, you guys stay here. I'll come in some time. Angira, come with me,' Iona starts mentally mugging up the Gujarati words that she had learnt from one of her Gujarati friends.

'Are you sure you want to do this?' Angira walks fast, trying to match Iona's pace.

'Let's try, we might just get some passes,' she says with a smile.

They reach the counter and ask for the passes. Before the guy at the counter can reply, the other guy standing near the counter says, '₹1,100.'

'I need two passes, sorry, three passes.'

'₹3,300,' he says.

'Bhai, bargaam thi avyo chu ane bav moto fan chu garba no... thaye toh trana pass nu kai adjust kar,' Iona speaks. Angira looks at him and says, 'Adjust kar...'

The person looks at both of them.

'Okay, come with me,' he says and takes them to the corner of the ticket counter and gives them three passes for ₹1,500.

'I can't believe you spoke in Gujarati,' Angira says gleefully.

'I hope I spoke correctly,' Iona answers.

'Whatever you did worked! By the way, what did you say to them?' Angira asks.

'I have come from out of town and I am the biggest fan of garba. Can you please give me three passes?' She giggles. 'I think I spoke it correctly.'

Upon overhearing them, few people around look at them.

Over the Limit, under Arrest

Timpanists are playing their drums full of energy, wearing kafni pyjama and dhoti. The women's dresses consist of colourfully embroidered designs and bare-backed blouses extending to the waist. They are wearing multi-coloured chaniya choli, ghagra, lehenga, saree or lancha. They look gorgeous, striking and stunning, and the dresses compliment their waist.

Charu is wearing a ghagra and her slim waist is grabbing everyone's attention. Anushka wears a kurti and churidar. She always looks beautiful because of the way she carries herself in any outfit. Iona is wearing a red kurta with white slacks. They are all looking colourful and beautiful.

While Iona and Angira have gone to get passes, Charu asks Anushka about Ved.

'When is Ved reaching? It's already 8 p.m.'

Anushka dials his number and waits for him to answer the call.

'Ved is not answering,' she says, redialling

'Do you have any other number?' Charu asks, pinging him on WhatsApp and checking to see when the tick marks turn blue.

'Messages are not even getting delivered,' Charu says.

Anushka steps away from the crowd and sees Iona and Angira coming.

'You guys go inside. I'll just come in a few minutes.'

'Are you sure?' Charu confirms if she needs any help.

'Yeah, yeah, I am fine. I'll just call Ved and come with him.

'Your pass?' Charu asks her

'I have it,' Anushka replies. She redials him and this time he answers.

Anushka waves her hand standing across the road and tells them she will come in ten minutes.

'Hello Ved, where are you?' Anushka almost shouts at him.

People are staring at her as she is looking terribly worried.

'This is Jignesh. We'll come in some time.'

'Where is Ved?' Anushka starts walking away.

'He is at the police station,' Jignesh says in a low voice.

'What? What happened to him?' Anushka is shocked.

'Nothing. Don't worry, we'll manage. Have you guys reached?' he asks her.

Ved and Jignesh have been at the Kandivali police station for the past half an hour.

'We have reached, but what happened? Give the phone to Ved,' Anushka shouts.

A man walking past her looks at her.

'He is inside. He gave me the phone to talk to you. Actually, we were on our way when our car broke down, so we asked for help from a policeman nearby. He took us to the police station saying that Ved is drunk. Now he is asking for ₹5,000 to let him go. We only have ₹3,000 on us. Let's see,' Jignesh peeps in through the window to where Ved is sitting and filling a form.

While Jignesh and Anushka are talking over the phone, Ved comes outside smiling, says, 'Done. Let's go.'

'Anushka,' Jignesh says.

He takes the phone.

'Abby, we are reaching in twenty minutes,' Ved says over the call like nothing happened.

'Ved, I am going to kill you. Are you okay?' Anushka is calm now.

'Yeah, I am fine. I just asked for help and he took me to the police station,' Ved says, acting like the most innocent guy Anushka has ever talked to.

'Because you are drunk. When are you reaching? Ask Jignesh to drive the car.'

'No, it's not me. It's Arjun and his unlucky car. Jignesh is fixing the problem. It isn't starting due to overheating. It's not far away. Maximum fifteen minutes.'

'Okay, come safely. Call me once you reach here and tell Jignesh to drive, okay?' Anushka gives him all the instructions to follow.

'Okay.'

Meanwhile Anushka calls Charu at the entry gate because she doesn't know how long Ved is going to take to reach. Instead of standing by the roadside, she decides to walk inside the venue. On the way to the entrance, Charu joins her and now they are busy discussing some steps in garba.

'Hey, come, come,' Charu says, reaching the crowd.

'Where is everyone?' Anushka asks Charu, trying to look for the others in the crowd.

Anushka looks tired and thirsty. She tries to look for drinking water.

'Angira just called me, was asking about Ved...' but she keeps quiet knowing she must not say anything about Angira and him. 'Hey, do you have a water bottle,' she asks Charu.

Charu picks up a bottle from a corner, where some girls have left their sandals and heels, and hands it to her.

'Is this ours?'

'No rights on water. Now have some and let's go,' Charu winks and pulls her into a huge circle of more than fifty people moving counter clockwise.

The basic dance formation is that of a circle that moves counter clockwise, four steps forward and two backward and is called popat. Charu points at Iona and Angira who are in the same circle. Their steps look well-rehearsed, while Anushka is trying hard to learn the steps, which doesn't stop her from enjoying the whole time. Angira looks damn funny while following those steps. These Gujju guys holding her hands on both sides have realized that she is new to the dance, so they try to teach her some of the steps. As the steps are rhythmic and repetitive, Angira can easily follow the beats and learn quickly.

Anushka receives a message on WhatsApp that Ved and Jignesh are reaching in five minutes.

'Not bad,' Ved shouts in the crowd.

Everyone is lost in the crowd and Anushka can only see Ved and his few friends walking toward her. Ved runs towards Anushka who is standing in the corner, tired, thirsty and sweating.

'This is Jignesh, my saviour of the day. Jignesh, this is Anushka, my friend,' Ved introduces them.

'Where is Charu?' he enquires.

He, in fact, wants to know where Angira is.

'How do you know Charu?' Anushka asks him.

Ved pauses and then responds, 'Angira called Arjun, so he told me that she is living with Charu.'

'Okay, she was just there in the circle,' Anushka tries to find her but she can't.

'Ved, did you keep water bottles in the car?' Anushka asks, hoping to get one from him.

'I think so,' Ved says, 'By the way, why have you called Iona here?'

'Ved, it's been more than two years. Why do you still hate her?'

'Because she deserves it.'

Ved wants to say more, but Charu waves at him from the other side. He waves back.

'Ved...'

'Okay, chill. Charu is coming,' Ved says to Anushka.

It is not as humid as it was when they arrived, but Ved desperately needs some cold water.

'Okay, I am going to get a bottle of water from the car. You guys carry on,' Ved assures them.

Anushka is worried about what will happen when Ved and Iona see each other.

No Replay, No Rewind

'Anu, I need water,' Angira says heavily panting. 'Bottle...,' she looks around.

Angira is searching for Ved in the crowd but she cannot find him anywhere.

'We can get it from the stall, but I left my wallet in the car,' Anushka says. Call Ved. He has gone to get a bottle of water. Tell him to get a few packets of chips as well,' Anushka sits on the floor wiping her face with a handkerchief. 'Get my wallet as well, if you can find it on the front seat. Should I come with you?'

'No, I'll get it,' Angira says, dialling his number.

Angira is tired and drags herself to the parking zone, which she takes time to find. Being afraid of the dark, Angira is scared as the parking lot has only one halogen light glowing in the distance. She wonders how a parking space this big is left unguarded. She calls Ved. Though his phone rings, he does not answer. She feels Ved must have gone back to the venue. She checks the side of the parking lot where Anushka said Ved has parked the car. She walks till the end and finally locates the car. As she walks towards the car, she hears some faint noises. She realizes there is someone else around the car and is scared. As the car comes into clear view, she sees Ved inside kissing a girl whose face she can't recognise in the dark. She suddenly feels empty and is unable to understand what to do next. She is in denial of what she just saw. However, she looks again and confirms it. She is in complete shock and remains silent. She doesn't know how to face this situation. *How can Ved do this to me*?

Should she drag Ved out of the car and give him a hard slap for fooling her for the last three months or go back to the venue? She hates this moment and never thought that Ved could do this to her. Questions are piling up in her mind, questions that go unanswered. She realizes the reason he was hiding his phone and why he deleted the

WhatsApp chat when she took his phone from him. In utter disbelief, she runs back to her friends who are waiting for her.

'What happened? I was looking for you, Angira. Why were you not answering my call?' Anushka asks her when she spots Angira at the exit.

'Nothing, I just got scared in dark. Where is Charu?' she asks and pretends as if nothing happened.

'What happened?' Anushka asks her.

'I am not feeling well, I want to go home.'

'You are sweating. Are you okay?'

'Is everything okay,' a person passing by asks Anushka.

'Yeah, fine,' she says. 'May I have your bottle of water?' She takes the bottle and gives it to Angira.

'Yeah, I am fine,' Angira says. 'Just felt a little weak...'

'I thought so. Did you find Ved?' Anushka asks her as they walk back to the area where people are dancing.

'No,' Angira says.

Angira is sitting on the floor and the events of the night flood her mind. She still doesn't believe what she saw.

'Where are Charu and Iona?' Angira wants to talk to Charu.

'They were there a moment ago. Wait, let me call them,' Anushka says and takes her phone out.

'No, that's okay.'

'Where is Ved?' Jignesh asks both of them. 'I can drop you home if you are not well.'

'Can you call Ved and ask if he can drop me,' Angira says, though right now she hates him the most.

'I am not feeling well. I want to go home,' Angira says and tries hard to control her tears because she could break down any moment and tell Anushka about how Ved has ruined everything.

Why do I always have to suffer? A drop of tear rolls down her cheek and mixes with the water she splashed on her face.

'Okay, let's go,' Anushka says.

'No, you stay here with them. Ved will drop me,' Angira replies, still thinking about what she saw in the car.

Ved appears.

'Are you okay?' Anushka asks her.

'Where were you?' Anushka asks Ved.

'Had gone out. I'll drop you,' he says.

Anushka realizes how messed up things are without Arjun. 'Sure you can drive?'

'Yes, I can drive, don't worry,' Ved says, though he doesn't look like he can.

Was it really Ved? Angira is feeling a pang of regret for not having knocked on the door of the car and caught him red-handed.

'Are you sure? Because I can come with you if you want,' Anushka asks her.

'No, I'll go,' she says.

'Okay, take care and text me once you reach,' Anushka waits until they leave.

'What happened to you?' Ved asks, looking at her.

'Nothing, can you drop me home?'

'Are you okay?' he asks her again.

'Yeah, I am fine.'

Ved drives the car and the moment she gets in, she start crying. She was the one who fell in love with a jerk and now she has to face the consequences. She can't even discuss this with Anushka because she will be asked to come back to Delhi to avoid what she went through earlier.

'What happened, Angira?' Ved senses something's wrong and stops the car.

'Can you please drop me home and cut the crap,' Angira says angrily.

She is in a solitary place of hopelessness, of a profound sadness and loss. Everything seems out of reach and she just is; she just exists. She feels a deep ache within that can't be shared with anyone.

'What happened?' he asks as if nothing happened a few minutes ago.

Ved realizes something serious has happened and this realisation is visible on his face. He still believes that he can make everything okay but she has already seen him betraying her.

'Ved, can you give me your phone?' she says rudely, looking outside the window.

She can't even look into his eyes anymore. There are moments when you know the person is guilty but you feel reluctant and avoid looking at them. Regret is the biggest teacher. She will make him regret what he has done.

'Why? What happened?'

'Can you please give me your phone?' she says again, seething with rage.

'No, first tell me what happened,' Ved still tries to normalize the situation.

'Then who was in your car? Tell me,' she shouts.

'Angira, calm down. We are on the road. Why are you making a scene over here?' he tries to placate her.

'Who was in the car?' she repeats, coming close to him like she is about to slap him.

'Nobody was there, Angira. Please listen to me. Let's go home and then we can talk,' Ved repeats.

He feels helpless. Angira walks out of the car and slams the door.

'Ved, I am not a roadside bitch. Never show me your face again. I am a Punjabi girl and I'll fuck you for your deeds, okay,' Angira kicks the car.

Ved tries to stop her, but she isn't in the mood to listen to anything. She calls Anushka and tells her that Ved is drunk and cannot drive her home. Then she switches off her phone and takes an autorickshaw home.

❧

It's early morning. Birds aren't chattering and the sun hasn't shown itself yet when Anushka leaves for Delhi.

After months Angira has woken up so early without an alarm. She feels numb and a strange unease has engulfed her. She comes out of her room and opens the window. She still feels suffocated. The air is heavy with gloom. She finds it difficult to breathe.

But why did he do something like this to me?

Was he with Charu? she starts thinking of every possibility.

Is this true?

Was it Charu in the car?

Angira goes into Charu's room, but she is fast asleep. She takes her cellphone and tries a few patterns to unlock her phone. She's successful in unlocking it, but she finds nothing related to Ved. Just a few old WhatsApp messages about her birthday.

She decides to confront Ved about his actions last night.

Is this the only way to know the truth about him? Or is there another way to find out who the girl is and ask her the truth?

She opens her Facebook account and searches for Ved's profile to check comments or likes on his photographs. Maybe she can get to know who that girl might be. She is not able to find anything and when she tries to find other pictures of Ved, she realizes that he has blocked her.

What the fuck has this bastard done?

She knows the username and password of Anushka's Facebook account. Everything is fair when you are in deep trouble. She logs in and goes through each and every picture that Ved has posted. It is almost impossible to check every profile of those who have liked and commented on his posts and pictures as there are thousands of them. Ved has numerous friends because of his game.

The gamer. The bastard. The cheater.

Is this love? Do I deserve this? Why the hell did I trust him? He just sleeps with every girl and spends his nights fucking around.

Before she does anything, she wants to call Ved and ask him why he cheated on her but his number is unavailable.

Has he blocked my number? she thinks and dials his number again but nothing changes. Then she realizes that either Ved must have left for Kolkata for his team selection process or he has blocked her.

Has he really gone for a stupid team selection process or to fuck around with more girls?

An intense pain and fear fills her as she is not ready to accept that Ved has cheated on her and left her all alone. There are pop ups of unread emails from last night on her phone. She opens her Gmail account and her eyes directly go to the email that Ved sent three hours after their fight.

She opens the email and starts reading. It says:

Hi Angira,

Please read this email patiently. I know, it's cowardly of me to send you an email rather than calling or meeting you to say what I have wanted to say since the last few days.

You are the kind of girl that any guy would go for, but I want to say something that I have felt over the last few months with you. You loved me truly and I always tried to love you back, but I just enjoyed your presence when you were physically close to me. Physical closeness is important in any relationship and you were the best at it, but I always felt the need to be alone after coming close physically rather than holding you in my arms and felt guilty having you around for just this purpose.

Angira, I may look happy but I am not really happy within. I have a family that is suffering. I have to do something for them. I know you won't forgive me for this, but our relationship was just an infatuation.

What if we wouldn't find happiness after years of being together?

I wanted to share lots of things with you but every time things happened and we just ended up getting physically intimate. The nights we spent together left me deeply unhappy because I have someone else in my life. I know this will hurt you and it hurts me to even say it, but it's better to make things clear.

I had told you about my previous relationship. She was my best friend. We became close again and realized that we still loved each other. I haven't cheated on you. Trust me, I was in love with you. I always pushed this relationship towards a good future, but now I find it is a hopeless cause.

I don't blame you in any manner and consider myself the culprit. I did try my best to love you but failed.

I respect that you have changed a lot for me. But we can't be with each other because I can't play with your feelings. I can only request you to go away from my life. There are some things I want to do with my life and I don't want to be distracted.

I know it's tough for you, please know that it's not easy for me either. But we need to accept that we can't be with each other. We follow different religions and it is something your family won't agree with. So rather than crying later, let's accept this fact today.

I am leaving for Kolkata in the morning. I'm very close to fulfilling my dream and I hope things will turn out okay after this.

Take care of yourself. You are a nice girl; you will get many great guys in the future.

Please don't contact me in any way. I have blocked you from everywhere: WhatsApp, Facebook and everywhere else. There is no future for us. We need to accept that.
Good luck to you.

Warm regards,
Ved Gulati

Angira is in tears. She doesn't know what to do now or how to react to this. She wants to call Ved and beg him not to leave her when everything around seems to be collapsing. Life comes full circle, as everything she faced in the past when her ex guy left her is happening to her all over again.

She dials his number but he is not reachable. Her lips are quivering as she feels numbness take over her body. She starts crying in her room and screams till her lungs hurt. She kneels on the floor and pleads, 'Please don't go away, please...I love you truly. Please don't go away...How can you do this to me?'

There is no one in the room to listen to her cries. She tries some numbers but nobody answers her calls. She holds both her hands as if in prayer and bangs her own head on the side of the bed.

Why? I never did anything wrong to anybody, then why am I suffering?

She cries uncontrollably, tears streaming down her face. Angira is beyond repair as her heart is breaking for the second time.

She dials Arjun's number and then stops. What will she tell him? He doesn't know anything about them. She decides against calling him.

She assumed that Charu was the culprit, but after reading the email it is clear that Charu was not with him. Then who was?

The birds are chattering now and the sun has risen but everything is gloomy in her life now. She cries for so long that she doesn't realize when she falls asleep. She wakes up after an hour and goes downstairs to get a cigarette. She gave up the things Ved did not like about her. Today she needs something to bust her stress.

There Can Never Be Another You

Angira has known that the first love is always about emotions and feelings. The second love is about maturity, and if love is found a third time, it is about compromises. Falling in love felt right to her, but it was a mistake she made twice and has to suffer for it. She has been lying in bed since morning. Charu tries to wake her up but she looks unwell, so she lets her sleep.

It is 8.15 p.m. when Angira wakes up. She feels the darkness around her and fears that it will soon swallow her. Sitting with her head buried in her hands, she rocks back and forth, sobbing inconsolably. She wraps her arms tightly around herself in a hug, hoping to comfort herself and puts her head on her knees. Her cheeks are stained with the endless stream of tears. She closes her eyes tightly and feels as if she's choking.

Standing at the window of her room, she remembers everything and lights the last cigarette.

'Angira, what the hell are you doing? Are you smoking?' Charu takes the cigarette from her hand and throws it out the balcony.

'You had quit, right?' Charu is seeing her smoking after many years. She senses that something is wrong.

'Is everything okay?' she asks.

Angira hugs her tightly and starts crying.

'Don't cry...don't cry. What is it? I am here, tell me what happened,' she hugs her tightly and pats her back.

'I'm sorry I doubted you. I'm really sorry,' Angira begs her.

'That's okay. But what happened, baby?'

She holds her chin, pulls it up a bit and looks into her bloodshot eyes. Charu asks her again and Angira tells her everything that happened since yesterday, including the email she read this morning. Charu calls Ved from her phone but it's still unreachable.

'I can't live without him. What did I do wrong? I can't live like this, please...' Angira cries her heart out. 'I will change myself if I have to. I was going to tell Anushka about him and...'

'You have to get a grip over yourself. He is not worth it. If he behaves like this, he is not the right guy for you. Why punish yourself? You have to come out of it, Angira. Everything will be fine, don't worry. Don't cry, my bachcha.'

Charu hugs her tightly in her arms and consoles her. She is the source of courage and support when Angira is completely shattered.

They both sit on the sofa. Charu hugs her and wipes her tears. Angira doesn't say a word. She releases herself from the hug and looks around. Every little place in the apartment has a memory of Ved that hurts her even more.

Charu makes her rest for some time. Without it, Angira might fall ill.

~

After an hour Charu comes in her room. She is still trying Ved's number to clear things out between them. She cannot believe that a guy like Ved can do this to Angira. He is just like all the other guys who go away, leaving someone behind with a broken heart.

'Angira, let's go and have dinner,' Charu insists.

'You eat. I am not hungry. I will eat after some time,' Angira says, ending the conversation.

She checks his WhatsApp profile and finds a display picture of him in Kolkata. She blocks him on WhatsApp.

'Angira, don't behave like this. You're the one who says that things change with time, even people do. So just forget whatever happened. You left everything you thought he won't like, but now you have started smoking. Are you not being selfish? Do you know how much Aunty and Anushka suffered because of you?' Charu tries to reason with her.

'Charu, can we talk sometime later? I really don't want to talk right now,' Angira gets up and goes to the other room, closing the door behind her.

'And what is this?' Charu shows her the packet of condoms that she found yesterday while putting her bag inside the cupboard.

She stops, suddenly realizing that she shouldn't interfere too much in Angira's personal life. But Charu also knows that it is a serious matter and she has to do something about it.

'Angira, did you tell Anushka about it?' Charu knocks the door and opens it.

Angira is frustrated that Charu won't stop talking.

'Please shut the fuck up! I am not hungry, why don't you understand? If you are hungry then go eat, but leave me alone for some time please,' Angira shouts at her.

Throwing herself on the bed she puts a pillow on her head.

Charu angrily shuts the door in the same way Angira did. She is hurt by the way Angira spoke to her.

'Fine, do whatever you want but remember, whatever you are doing is not right. You won't accept that you are doing anything wrong because the situation is not in your favour. Just think once before you do something stupid. There are lots of guys around, so it all depends on how you deal with it. There is food in the kitchen, have if you feel like, otherwise leave it for tomorrow. Please inform me beforehand, so I won't cook for you.'

Charu is aware that Angira is hurting but she is deeply hurt by Angira's words. She knows that Angira discusses everything with her but recent events have brought a sense of negativity and distance between them. She is concerned about Angira and wants to tell Anushka everything but doesn't. If they come to know, they won't trust Angira anymore. Angira has promised her family that she will not create any more problem for them, especially while she is in Mumbai.

Angira has hardly eaten since yesterday and cried throughout the day and the whole night. She has noticed that when Angira gets hungry, she goes to the kitchen in the middle of the night, takes a bite of food, and just chews on it for a long time sitting in the hall. When Charu opens the door of her room, she pretends that she's asleep and cries as soon as the door closes.

Is this the life I deserve? What did I do wrong in my life? Angira continues to question herself. She keeps checking her phone though there are no calls or messages on it. It seems everything has vanished—her dreams, her happiness, the future she had imagined with Ved. She is not talking to Charu and she has told her that she needs time and does not want anyone to interfere. She has started isolating herself. When her college friends call to know why she is not coming to college, she does not answer their calls. Moreover, Charu has to pretend that Angira has gone back to Delhi for few days and will be back next week. She repeats the same when they call again the next day. Angira looks weak and tired. Initially she ignored people; now people have started ignoring her. Nobody likes to sit with her or talk to her. One can look so different in the matter of a few days, Charu observes. Angira was on medication, but she has stopped taking them now. It seems she is going further into depression.

Angira listens to Arjun and respects his advice. Hoping that he can help her, Charu calls him one evening without telling Angira because she cannot stand Angira's negativity at home.

'Hi, who's this?' Arjun enquires.

'Hey Arjun, this is Charu. Where are you?'

'Hi Charu, how are you? I am in Mumbai. Tell me,' Arjun says, but he guesses that something serious must've happened as Charu has never called him before.

'Is Ved around?' Charu asks him.

'You know him?' Arjun asks her.

'Angira told me about him,' Charu says and asks, 'Is he there?'

'No, he has gone to Kolkata,' he says and enquires, 'Why? What happened?'

'Nothing. I want to talk to you.'

'Yes, what happened? Is everything fine?'

'No, nothing is fine. Did Angira tell you anything?'

'No, what happened? She used to send me jokes on WhatsApp, but she has not said anything since the last few days, so I figured she might be busy with work,' Arjun is perceptive.

The first thought that comes in his mind is that her mom was unwell since last few weeks.

'Ved cheated on her and now she is not her senses anymore. She is going into depression. She has stopped eating,' Charu tells him everything she knows and asks him come home and talk to Angira.

Initially, he finds it hard to comprehend as he still doesn't know much about the equation between Ved and Angira. He is surprised but also hurt that neither Ved nor Angira discussed anything with him. However, this is not the time to react.

'Where is she now?' he enquires. 'Does Anushka know about this?'

'She is home. She doesn't know that I have called you. No, Anushka doesn't know about this. She didn't tell anybody. She is completely broken right now. If possible, come soon and try to make her understand. She listens to you,' Charu says.

'Don't worry, I will reach there in some time. Just text me the address,' Arjun says.

It's 9.30 p.m. and Arjun rushes off in his car. He thinks for a moment. He wants to call Ved but doesn't because Angira needs him more right now. Though Ved has never wronged Arjun, he is suddenly reminded of the time during their college days when Ved was accused of attempting rape. Arjun connects the dots and vows to make Ved suffer for his mistakes. The guy who used to love her more than anything, left her alone crying all night. Arjun is worried sick about Angira.

~

Arjun reaches her apartment at 10.15 p.m. Charu takes him inside while Angira is having dinner in the hall.

'Hello,' Arjun surprises her.

Angira gets up.

She wonders why Arjun has come to her apartment now, considering he never came before when she had invited him for a party. Some people will not be with us when we need to celebrate but will be there with us in our dreadful times. Arjun is one of them. Angira is happy to see him, but she does not know where to begin telling him about everything that has happened.

'Hey, how are you?' she asks.

'I am good. How you are doing? Take your time,' Arjun says, smiling at the way she is eating in a hurry.

'No, I am done,' she replies, still chewing.

Arjun takes the water bottle from the dining table and sits on the sofa with Charu next to him.

It's apparent on both their faces that Angira and Charu aren't talking much.

'I'll be back in two minutes,' Angira goes in her room to change.

Arjun guesses from Angira's appearance that she is going through depression. He is sitting on the sofa from where he can easily see her room. He can see unwashed clothes dumped in the corner of the bed, unwashed glasses lying on the floor. It's not clearly visible but he finds wrappers of medicines and chart paper of the same colour that he saw Ved use a few weeks ago. Probably cards, Arjun assumes. He prefers to go in her room rather than talking to her like any other friend would. Today she needs a sister in Arjun so she can shout, cry and talk about everything that's bothering her. Sometimes you can't discuss some things with girls and boys would understand those issues better. Arjun has to be there for her.

'May I come in?' he asks.

'Hey, yes sure,' Angira speaks from the other corner without looking at him. She appears to be wiping her face with a towel. She looks much better than she did the time Arjun entered, though the dark circles are still visible under her eyes.

'Thanks.'

Arjun sits on her bed. She starts clearing everything from the bed.

'Things which have piled up take time to be cleared. You can't do everything in one shot. Leave it, it's perfectly fine,' he says and smiles at her

Angira still moves everything in the corner and clears the bed. Arjun notices a small row of photos hanging on the front wall. The paint is a little weathered and peeling off in places, and the shutters on the windows next to the wall are mostly dusty. A slight breeze makes the shutters tap against the hose and the hinges squeak.

'It's good of you to come,' Angira says offhandedly, just to start a conversation.

'Yes, I felt like meeting you,' he smiles.

'Charu gave you the address?' she asks him.

'I am here now, that's the important thing.'

'Okay, what would you like to have,' she asks him and comes closer to Arjun to pick up the card which is lying near his legs in the corner of the bed.

Arjun takes it in his hand and says, 'That's okay, let it be.'

He puts it on the bed. Angira looks ill, the exhaustion clearly visible on her face. She has figured out that Charu has told Arjun about her and Ved. Angira nods, smiling, though she is suffering on the inside.

'You don't need to pretend,' Arjun says to Angira. 'So how are you?' he asks her, sipping some water.

'Arjun, do you really believe that true love exists?' she asks him.

'Yes, I do.'

'And you?' he asks her.

'I used to when I was in school. Someone came into my life and broke me into pieces, and then I had no faith in love. It's all about having sex,' she says, realising she has spoken too much.

Her eyes are full of tears now.

'And you know when you came home in Delhi that time and said so much about love and life, I didn't trust you initially. But Anushka told me to spend some time with you because you are full of positive energy. Your words inspired me and I started believing whatever you said. It's good to hear that someone will come into your life and will love you forever and blah...but in reality it almost never happens. When I came to Mumbai, I met Ved and everything changed in my life. Just when I had started believing in love, he ditched me and ran away without telling me. I changed myself for him. I thought of telling you about him but he just...'

Angira wipes her tears and presses her lips. She tries hard to stop her tears but she cannot. How can she forget those days when she cooked for him, waited for him after the class at the bus stop for hours. She shared the same drink, the same piece of bread and even the same bed for several nights. How can she forget those days?

'Angira, I still don't know what happened between you and Ved, because he called me in the evening and asked about you. I wondered how he knew about you. Then he told me everything. He said he tried to call you, but you are not reachable.'

'Why the hell is he calling you now? He is an asshole! He was just passing time with me and I didn't even realize it for a moment. I blame you too. You didn't tell me about him,' Angira is frustrated. The more she speaks, the more she hurts herself.

'You never told me that Ved and you are in a relationship. Even Anushka didn't tell me anything,' Arjun says. His words show that he was expecting more from Anushka and Angira. Expectations hurt. He realizes this time and again.

Charu comes in, 'Is everything okay.'

Arjun nods.

'Hey Arjun, you want something to eat? You must be hungry,' Charu interrupts.

'No, I am stuffed.'

'Don't worry, I will make you a quick bite.'

Charu goes out of the room. Maybe she is feeling a little ignored as Arjun and Angira have been talking for quite some time now. She turns back and looks inside the room. She smiles looking at Arjun and he smiles back.

'But what happened,' he asks Angira again.

Angira tells him everything that happened in the parking lot when Ved was kissing an unknown girl in the car and the email Ved sent her.

'I don't know what to say, but let me talk to Ved once. I want to talk to him now,' Arjun is full of anger.

He is hurt, especially because Angira blamed him, but he understands her situation.

'I suspected this,' Arjun murmurs.

'What?' Angira asks him.

'Nothing...'

'Arjun, are you hiding something?'

Holding two plates of noodles in her hand, Charu enters the room, 'Here, eat.'

Arjun takes the newspaper and keeps a plate on that.

'Hold! Hold! It's hot,' Charu hands Angira the other plate.

Angira gets up partially and holds the plate. Arjun finishes the noodles and texts Ved on WhatsApp. He is waiting for the message to get delivered.

'Okay, I have to go, it's 11.45 p.m.' Arjun gets up after having a few sips of water.

Questions that weigh heavy on his mind still need to be resolved. Arjun gives her a hug and she really needs it from the way she holds on to him a little longer.

'Everything will be all right.'

Angira feels safe when Arjun is around her. Whenever she talks to him, she accepts whatever he says. His presence has made her feel a little better. However, not much has changed today.

Why did I fall for Ved of all people? she thinks for a moment and then wishes, *I wish I could have a guy like Arjun, who could solve everything so easily.*

'Good night,' Arjun waves and leaves.

Angira comes back to bed, puts her head under a pillow and pretends to be asleep when Charu comes around.

Flight SE786 to Destiny

Arjun is lying in bed, reducing and then increasing the temperature of the air conditioner. He logs on to his Facebook account to check Ved's profile and scrolls all the way down but doesn't find anything suspicious. Only one person has liked every photograph that Ved posted and that is Angira.

He takes his cellphone and sends him a message again.

Hi Ved, where are you? Need to talk about something urgent.

Arjun checks the message that he has sent. The message has been delivered.

What happened?
Is everything fine?

I just called Angira,
Her number is still not reachable.

I just got back from her place.
She has blocked you because of your deeds.

What???
I am calling you.

Next moment, the phone rings and Arjun receives his call.

'What happened? Why did she block me?'

'Because you cheated on her and she caught you. You told me some things about that evening but why didn't you tell me what you were doing with a girl in the car? What are you doing with other girls? And what you have emailed her? Really Ved, what's going on? She has tried to commit suicide once before because of her previous relationship, do you know that? You don't know that because you don't know her. She's much better than what you deserve,' Arjun shouts at Ved.

Arjun cares a lot about Angira, especially because she is Anushka's younger sister. Arjun doesn't know what role he needs to play right now but he was always there for Anushka, and after meeting Angira, he equally cares for her.

'What are you saying?' Ved asks.

Arjun interrupts, 'Ved, if anything happens to her, you will be solely responsible. You were blamed for the rape attempt in college, now I doubt that...'

'Arjun, shut the fuck up right now! Don't accuse me of things I haven't done. I have not done anything. Why are you always angry with me? What grudges do you still have with me even after four years of college? I moved into your place because Anushka told me to and for the last six months you have been acting weird with me. If there is anything you want to say, just say it directly to me,' Ved shouts back at him.

Arjun does not reply.

Ved continues, 'And I didn't rape anyone, okay. If you want me to leave your place, I'll do that once I'm back. But please stop talking rubbish because I can't hear all this fucking nonsense anymore. And if you are not talking to me because of someone else then it's your problem. Iona was your best friend before she blamed me for no fucking reason.'

Arjun is surprised at the sudden mention of Iona in the conversation.

Ved continues, 'I haven't done anything, Arjun. You and Anushka know this very well, right? Don't you? Moreover, if you still had doubts about me then why didn't you discuss it with me? Arjun, I have tried hundreds of times to discuss this with you and Anushka. I hope she has understood me, but you haven't even tried to because you have become so involved in your work. You only look at things from the perspective of profit and loss. You can tell me whatever you want at home, face-to-face. And as for my advice—take some time out for your friends and family. This is just a suggestion for you,' Ved is frustrated.

'Dude, I'm not interested in listening to any of this. I haven't called you to ask for advice. I know what to do and how to do it. Charu called me over, stating that Angira is depressed. She was on medication which you must know very well. She saw you with some girl in the car on garba night. Is she lying?' Arjun questions him.

Arjun recalls everything that Angira told him about the garba night. Ved calms down and listens to him, then responds because he knows he has made a mistake that he'll regret forever.

'I don't know what she has told you, but I wanted to talk to Angira and Anushka about Iona that night. But at the time Angira wasn't in the mood to listen. She was shouting on the roadside and I didn't want to make a scene over there. I tried calling her but her number was not reachable and next day I had to leave for Kolkata. I tried calling Charu also, but she didn't respond to any of my calls. What has she told you?' Ved asks her.

Ved wishes that he could resolve everything immediately. He is afraid of losing Angira.

'So who were you with in the car that day,' Arjun asks him again.

He suspects Iona as Ved has suddenly spoken about her. He is reminded of the days when Iona and Ved were in college. They were more than classmates back then.

'I was drunk and I accept my mistake,' Ved admits to his folly and proceeds to tell Arjun the whole story.

'That night, Iona wanted to talk. When we went to the parking area to get some water bottles, she followed me till the car and then requested me to talk for just a few minutes. She almost begged me. I agreed to talk and we went inside the car. She said she wanted to be with me and pleaded me to give her one more chance at a fresh start. I kept telling her that I love Angira and that Iona hasn't been in my life for the last four years. I only replied to her messages because I didn't want to be rude to her. That night while talking, she suddenly started kissing. I was drunk just as she was. I just could not avoid it for a few seconds. I just lost control physically. Iona had seen Angira coming close to the car and then everything went south.'

Ved wanted to discuss this with Angira but he just needed some time to come back from Kolkata. He knew once he is selected for the team, he would tell her the truth and everything would be all right.

Ved describes each and every thing to Arjun, who is stunned and remains silent.

'And that email you sent to Angira?' Ajrun confirms.

'I didn't send any email. I can't check my email because someone changed my password. So how can I possibly email her? Angira has blocked my number. I can't even contact her on Facebook or WhatsApp and you are shouting at me.'

Ved is thoroughly confused by what has happened.

'What did you tell Angira? Why did you go to her home at night? You could have called me first,' Ved shoots some questions.

'Do you doubt me?' Arjun is hurt.

He always treated Ved as his younger brother. Though he cares for Angira more than he does for Ved.

'I am not doubting you. But even her sister, Anushka, was saying that Angira liked you when she first met you. And which email are you are talking about?' Ved's voice reflects how frustrated he is.

'Ved, enough! I went to her home because she is not eating and is depressed. She is on medication. Now, just call her,' Arjun tells him about the email that Angira showed him.

Ved feels helpless.

Arjun calls Angira immediately.

'Hi Angira,' Arjun says over the call.

'What happened? Is everything okay? Why are you calling so late in the night?' Angira becomes mindful.

'I just had a talk with Ved. He was calling you. He says that he hasn't done anything wrong. He didn't send that email to you. He isn't able to access his email account and it seems that someone else is using it. He tried calling you on your number, but you have blocked him, even on Facebook and WhatsApp.'

'What? Are you sure?'

'He says that you blocked him on Facebook. I don't know what's going on between you guys, but you need to sort it out. He was crying as he spoke. He has called you several times, just listen to him once,' Arjun says and adds, 'I think he is not lying'

'And who was he with in the car?' Angira is listening to Arjun, but she suspects him for a moment as well. She doesn't trust anyone after what happened in last few days.

'He was with Iona.'

'What? What are you saying? How do you know that?'

Angira asks several questions out of anger and frustration.

'Yes, he was Iona,' Arjun explains her.

Arjun and Iona used to be best friends in college days. Anushka was a friend of Iona's, who was a year senior, and then Arjun met Anushka. Anushka used to help him most of the times because of his genuineness. Arjun stared sharing the same bond with Anushka that he shared with Iona. Ved was his classmate, and then later roommate in hostel. The four had become like a family. They celebrated late night birthdays, got drunk in the boy's hostel; back-slapping friends, numerous cups of tea on sleepless nights; so many stories and very little studying; it went on till the end of the very last semester. They used to sit together in the canteen, sharing food with each other. Though they were loaded with assignments and projects, they had fun in their own way. In the evening, they would go out for walks together; so much laughter, such happiness, no anger and no pride. Dinner was just an excuse to meet everyone at the same table. They enjoyed even in the classroom, where they teased the professors, threw pieces of chalk at each other, ate chocolates, bunked classes, went for movies and never listened to anyone. There was very little money but a lot of love.

During this beautiful journey, love blossomed between Ved and Iona, and very dramatically, Ved proposed to Iona on her birthday in the academic block in front of Anushka and Arjun. Many guys were after Iona but she chose Ved. They were madly in love and became the best couple in college.

Everything was going fine between Iona and Ved. One day, he came to know about one of her friends who was part of the mixed basketball team, of which Iona was the captain. Hate is a four-letter word. So is love. Sometimes we don't understand the difference between the two. Ved became possessive about her because Iona used to spend all her time with him on the basketball court. As the days passed, they started fighting. It was Christmas evening. Arjun and Anushka were back home. Iona and Ved were struggling to resolve things and their relationship was on the edge. She got frustrated and filed a case of sexual assault against him because he became very possessive and started enquiring about her whereabouts. He tried to resolve their issues but everything was so messed up that it eventually ruined their relationship. Ved came to know all of a sudden about this when the vice chancellor and registrar of college rusticated him for one semester.

They called Iona to withdraw the complaint and Ved also pleaded in front of her because this could ruin his career for a lifetime. Ved wrote in an affidavit that he would not talk to Iona while they are still in college. Eventually, he stopped talking to everyone. Rumours spread like fire in the college and everybody came to know that Iona filed a rape case against Ved. That was the worst year of college for Arjun, Anushka and Ved. Iona also stopped talking to Arjun because Ved was his roommate and she felt that everything had changed. Their own friends had a different perception of Ved and this impacted Arjun too because they were roommates. Arjun faced the consequences when he was asked to leave Ved, else he would ruin his career too, but Arjun knew Ved very well. So he tried to fix things and keep the group together but he failed. Their equation had changed. It was the last year of college; everyone got placements through college and left, but this group became a topic of gossip for their juniors forever.

'How can Iona do this to Ved?' Angira is emotional and hurt.

She feels sorry for him now and has started hating Iona. She is able to connect all the dots and is trying to recall if Iona gave her Ved's number intentionally at the party in Delhi. If yes, then why? She tells Arjun whatever she remembers and then he tells her that Iona and Ved have the same series of number. It was a craze in college for couples to have the same sequence of numbers. So they had similar numbers. Iona's was 90XXXXXX68 and Ved's ended with a 7 instead of an 8. So maybe that night when Iona gave her number to Angira, she mistyped it and her message went to Ved, which is how everything began.

'Shit, what the hell! She is such a bitch for trying to ruin me,' Angira says in a fit of rage. She continues, 'That's why when I told her about Ved over the call and showed her his picture, she didn't respond. I didn't know that she was such a devil. Should I call her and question her? I am not like the girls who just suffer and forget. I'll show her what I am and what I can do,' she says.

'Angira, calm down. Everything is fine now. Don't take stress,' Arjun tells her to take care of herself.

Angira is on medication and if she takes stress she will go into depression again.

'Did you tell Anushka about this?' Arjun asks her.

Anushka should know about them. It's high time. Angira needs her sister with whom she can share things and take this relationship ahead.

'No.'

'Then call her and tell her everything. Meanwhile, I will talk to Ved about his return,' Arjun says.

'Okay, but what about the email I received from Ved? Who sent it? And how?' Angira asks, still full of doubts and questions.

Though Angira is not prepared to face her sister, she decides to tell Anushka everything that happened on garba night. She calls her and tells her the whole story. Anushka is completely shocked after finding out that they had been in a relationship for over three months. She is afraid because she knows everything about Ved and his past. While Anushka is happy for her and thinks that his past should not hamper their relationship, she isn't fully convinced yet. Angira takes time to convince her and succeeds. Anushka finally understands that Ved is the right match for her. Now she has to help Angira in convincing their family, which is not an easy task. Before that, she has to talk to Ved about why Iona is still after him despite the fact that he has moved on.

'Okay, I'll call you later in the evening,' Angira tells Anushka over the call.

'Okay.'

'Don't tell mamma anything about it as of now,' Angira emphasizes on her last sentence before she disconnects the call.

'Okay.'

Angira unblocks his number and starts receiving the numerous messages on WhatsApp that Ved had sent to her.

It's all about our perception of things. She reads all the messages and wells up with tears. She realizes how grossly misunderstood Ved is.

She couldn't be happier and calls Arjun. Anushka has also assured her that Ved couldn't have done this to anyone as she has known him for years.

'What happened?' Arjun asks eagerly.

'I want to meet him,' Angira says excitedly over the call.

'What?' he asks.

'I want to meet him,' she repeats herself.

'But he is coming tomorrow, I just chatted with him,' Arjun smiles.

'No, tomorrow is far away, I want to surprise him. Please give me the address of the place he is staying at in Kolkata. I want to go there directly as I haven't called him yet.'

'At least call him once and inform him. And are you sure you want to go there? Have you visited Kolkata before?' Arjun asks, taken aback by Angira's impulsiveness. Then he smiles remembering the days when he used to do the same thing—travelling by trains for hours to meet his love.

In love, even a meeting of a few minutes can give one all the happiness in the world.

'No, I won't call. I will go and meet him. And I have been there before, so I won't face any problems. I have checked the flights as well and I am booking a ticket. Please don't tell him that I am coming to meet him.'

She quickly books a ticket for Kolkata. It's an early morning flight the next day.

'I am happy for you,' Arjun says.

'Thanks for everything, Arjun,' Angira says with a tone of gratitude.

'Okay, I'll text you the address where he is staying. Have a good time with him,' Arjun says with a smile.

'Thanks Arjun!' she says.

'You are lucky to have me,' Arjun laughs.

'Haha, so true! Bye, take care.'

'Bye.'

Angira disconnects the call and checks her phone for the ticket. She takes a grey jacket and rushes out of her home. She turns back to her room and takes out a bottle from her drawer. It's not a bottle of wine or vodka. It has hundreds of small colourful thermocol balls, with a message on a scroll tied-up with a red ribbon. It is capped with a golden fabric and tied-up with the same red ribbon. There is a small note hanging from the neck of the bottle. She smiles and puts it in her handbag.

'Where are you going so late? Are you okay?' Charu comes from her room. She has woken up from the hullabaloo in the hall for the past few hours.

'Going to Kolkata!' she jumps on Charu and hugs her.

'What happened?' Charu asks, though she figures she is going to meet Ved.

'I have troubled you a lot. Now I'll leave you in peace for some time,' Angira laughs.

'That you have done so many times,' Charu says sarcastically.

'If Anushka calls you, don't tell her that I am not home. For more information, call Arjun. I love you. Bye!' Angira takes her backpack and handbag and walks out the door.

She reaches the airport at the nick of time. She moves quick to get her boarding card and then walks towards the boarding gate. She realizes that Ved always hoped for some romantic gestures from her and now was her chance to give it her best shot. However, plans don't always go according to our will.

∞

Arjun wakes up to Ved's messages early in the morning. He misses going for a jog or for a swim with him.

Good morning. Sorry buddy, I shouted at you.
I was frustrated...hope you forgive me and allow me to enter the house :P

Arjun finds it hard to believe that Ved has texted him so early in the morning. He smiles reading his message on WhatsApp. It is not the first time that they have exchanged unkind words but this time, Ved was a little insensitive.

Chill dude, that's okay.
You had your reasons...

By the way, your dude is selected to play his next match for Kolkata :D

That's awesome!
Now, we'll have party!

Yes, we will all catch up over some drinks.

That you do anyway. This time something more ;)
By the way, I'm happy for you

Arjun is happy for him and feels like they never fought. He calls Ved.

'What's up, my love?'

'All well, my player, finally you rocked. I am proud of my son,' Arjun says with a smile. 'By the way, is that the reason you are up so early? Where are you?' Arjun hears some noise coming from the background and asks him. 'Enjoying a party with bong girls?'

Ved giggles.

'That I did last night.' He laughs and says, 'I am just going to catch my flight to Mumbai. Let's go out for lunch.'

'Weren't you supposed to come tomorrow?' Arjun asks. He is worried about Angira as she must have left for Kolkata by now.

'How could I wait until tomorrow to meet Angira? Anyway, it's today not tomorrow. I told you.'

'Angira has left for Kolkata to meet you and you are coming back to Mumbai! Call her and talk to her right now,' Arjun says.

'What?' Ved just stepped onto the flight.

'Yes.'

'Oh shit, let me call her,' Ved disconnects the call and calls Angira the next moment. He gets the automated response: the number you have dialled is not reachable at this moment, please try again later.

He calls again and gets the same response. He calls Arjun.

'Her phone is not reachable. I don't know what to do. I am on the flight and I can't de-board now.'

'Your flight goes via Bangalore, right?' Arjun asks him. He can hear the hostess asking Ved to switch off his phone.

'Yes. Is she coming via Bangalore too?' Ved asks him, and hiding himself from the hostess, he continues the conversation. 'What should I do now?'

'No, she is not coming via Bangalore,' Arjun says

Ved is panicking.

'Don't worry. Just call me once you reach Bangalore.'

'Tell me now,' Ved asks him impatiently.

The hostess requests him to switch off his phone, this time more sternly and with sharp words.

'You reach Bangalore and call me.'

As Angira can't take calls, Arjun drops her a message on WhatsApp requesting her to call him when she reaches Bangalore.

❧

Arjun gets a call from Angira after an hour. 'Hey, Arjun! How are you? I got your message just now, what happened?'

'I hope you are not travelling with heavy bags,' Arjun asks her.

'No, but why, what happened?' Angira asks in confusion.

'Ved has left for Mumbai and you have left for Kolkata,' Arjun says, going into the kitchen and taking out a water bottle from the refrigerator.

'Oh fuck! I should have called him before leaving,' Angira says regretfully.

'I had suggested that but you wanted to give him a surprise,' says Arjun.

'Why didn't you tell him about it before he left?'

'He had already boarded the flight by the time we spoke. Besides, you told me not to tell him that you are going to surprise him. You are lucky that you have a flight via Bangalore'

'What do I do now?'

She decides that once she reaches Kolkata, she can take the next flight back to Mumbai.

Arjun says, 'You can de-board at Bangalore.'

'Why?'

'I didn't tell him that your flight is also via Bangalore. He doesn't know you have a stoppage there, so you could totally surprise him in your way.'

'That's just great! Now I understand why people love you. You are the best at giving suggestions on romance,' she laughs, now turning towards the exit gate.

'Thanks a lot, Arjun! I must say, it's rare to find a friend like you.'

He laughs, saying, 'You're welcome!'

'Thanks a lot for being there for Ved and me,' Angira thanks him.

'Now call Ved once he reaches Bangalore,' Arjun says and goes back in his room, opens his diary and writes a few illegible lines.

Via-via

The weather is pleasant in Bangalore; it's almost as if nature is setting up the perfect ambience for a date for Angira and Ved. Sometimes the unexpected brings with it a lot of joy. Angira constantly tries Ved's number. It is unreachable. His flight hasn't landed in Bangalore yet. Time seems to be running slow. Angira has exited the airport.

She wonders, 'What if Ved doesn't switch on his phone and directly reaches Mumbai?'

Her own thoughts trouble her, but for obvious reasons. She tries calling him again, but his phone is still unreachable. She calls Arjun, but he seems to be busy as well.

'Why the hell is nobody picking up my calls?' Angira murmurs.

She now thinks of taking a flight to Mumbai. Her flight to Kolkata is about to leave. She is worried that she might not get a ticket to Mumbai. Finally, she decides to go to Kolkata. She knows she has a place to stay; her uncle's home. Once she reaches the security gate, the official asks her to hurry up.

'Ma'am, the flight is about to take off, hurry up!' says the person scanning the bag.

Saying thanks to him, Angira scampers to catch her flight. Breathing fast, she reaches the gate to board the flight. The final announcement is made for flight SE786. Angira is worried about the questions her parents will ask her about her trip to Kolkata. Her phone rings. She feigns illness and the security in-charge allows her to go out of the line.

'Hello Angira!'

'Hello, who is this?' she asks him.

'May I talk to Angira? I hope she remembers me,' Ved says.

'No, she does not want to...' Angira says, though she is feeling like she is the happiest person on earth right now.

Love doesn't demand preparation; it demands attention and purity of thoughts. In the same way, a girl never demands that one buys her precious gifts, except at some rare moments; she dreams of having a precious person in her life who can make any moment special for her.

'Okay, I'll remain on call. Once she is free, she can speak up,' says Ved.

Sniffing over the phone, she says, 'Shut up, where are you? Do you even care for me? At least you should've called me when things were going wrong. Arjun told me everything.'

'So, do you have any more doubts?' Ved asks her.

'No, now I know everything about you—from your past to your future,' Angira tells him, sounding joyous.

'Oh, the future too, huh? Where are you? And your voice has changed in just a week,' Ved tries to mock her, though he knows how important she is in his life.

'You have changed, not me. Now, come down to the lobby, I am waiting here,' Angira says, taking a few steps back to check if Ved is coming towards her.

She calls back and asks in anticipation, 'Where are you? I can't see you.'

'Right next to you,' Ved says, tapping on her shoulder from behind. 'Thanks to Arjun,' he adds.

'Oh really,' she says over the call.

Angira turns. The man standing in front of her has intense black eyes and is wearing blue denims with a white cotton shirt, which fits perfectly on his muscular body. The same shirt he wore when they first met at Juhu beach.

Ved sees her oval face, long eyelashes and her brown eyes glistening in the bright sunlight. Her hair, dark brown, falls messily over her shoulders. She looks even prettier as a light gust of wind makes some loose strands of hair fall across her cheeks. He had gifted her a pair of fish-shaped earrings that she is wearing right now and they really suit her face.

She jumps on Ved and hugs him tightly. He takes her in his arms. People walking by are looking at them. Madly in love, he ignores the commotion around them and kisses her passionately. They are lost in each other for a few minutes.

'I think people are staring at us now,' Ved says.

'Ignore them...I missed you a lot,' she sniffs.

'I missed you too.'

'I hate you,' Angira remembers whatever happened in the last few days.

'Well, I don't,' Ved hugs her more tightly and whispers into her ears.

'You are such a bad boy,' Angira says, her head resting on his shoulder.

'Maybe, but I know I am "the one" for you.'

'Shut up, people are staring at us,' Angira says, but they are still hugging each other.

'Ignore them.' Ved replies.

'You haven't changed a bit, even the fragrance of your body is the same,' Ved says, after which he is quiet for a while.

'What is it?' Angira asks and holds his hand.

'Nothing...let's not think of whatever happened in the last few days. We love each other and that's what's important,' Ved says.

'Let's go,' Angira says, holding him as they walk towards the exit of the lobby.

'But where are we going?' Ved slows down and looks at her for an answer.

'I don't want to go back to Mumbai so soon,' Angira replies, still unsure of where to go.

'Do you have any work to finish in Mumbai?' he asks.

'Not really. Let's stay here today and then we will go back tomorrow,' Angira says.

'That's what I was about to tell you,' Ved says, with a broad smile.

The foggy weather is followed by sunshine, and then comes the rain. Ved and Angira keep walking through it all and enjoy the beautiful Bangalore weather, which is just as pleasant throughout the year.

'I like this place, as always,' Ved says, walking in the light drizzle.

He remembers the first time when they met at Juhu beach and it was drizzling them too. Angira looks beautiful as she tucks her wet hair behind her ears.

'What are you staring at?' she waves her hand in front of his eyes.

'Nothing...is this a dream?' he beams.

'It's not a dream. It's raining and you're looking good,' she grins.

'Remember when we met at Juhu beach?' Angira brings exactly what Ved was thinking about just a moment ago.

'I do. Oh and I have some good news,' says Ved.

'What's that?' she asks curiously.

'I.'

'Am.'

'Selected for the Kolkata team!' Ved shares his most beautiful moment with her.

'I am in seventh heaven right now,' Angira jumps with happiness. Everything is just perfect.

The rain has made everything romantic for them, and looking into each other's eyes they kiss again. Holding each other by the road side, they forget the world around them, ignoring all the passers-by. Their eyes say what words cannot. Angira has questions that need to be answered, but today is not the day. Tomorrow they celebrate Ved's success with Arjun and the others, the rest will be taken care of later. For now, they cherish each other's company.

Unofficially Yours

Angira and Ved check into a hotel room late afternoon after roaming on the MG road. They will stay here for a day and then leave for Mumbai the next morning. Ved decides to throw a grand party next week. Arjun has been asked not to give excuses and join the celebrations.

'What are you doing?' Angira asks, taking the towel in her hand.

'Watching other girls,' Ved says in jest.

Ved is resetting the password of his Facebook and Gmail account.

'If you can't appreciate your girl, don't look at others,' Angira replies sarcastically.

'The opposite is also true, right?' Ved laughs.

He goes to the sent items of his email account and reads the mail which created a ruckus in his life. He deletes it and shuts down the laptop after changing the password.

'Shut up now,' Angira says, poking his waist. 'What are you thinking?' she asks him as he looks a little worried.

'Nothing,' Ved says, still wondering who could've sent this email. 'Is this Iona? But how?'

'Ved, may I ask one thing?' Angira looks curious. Ved understands what she is going to ask and is prepared for it.

'If you didn't send me that email, then who did?' she asks.

Though she is happy to have Ved back in her life, there are things she must know.

'Anushka and Iona are coming on Saturday, you will get your answer then,' Ved says confidently.

'Promise?'

'Promise.'

'Never leave me. I truly love you and I can't face a heartbreak again.'

Ved is lying on his stomach, when Angira comes and hugs him from the back.

'Is this a good position?' he says laughing.

'I'll kill you. Go away,' she punches him on his shoulder and gets up. 'I will come in ten minutes,' she adds.

She wraps the red towel around her neck and walks off to the bathroom. She is wearing a white shirt.

'Red and white suit you,' he says, looking at her.

She hoots and continues, 'And you are wearing white again.'

'That's my lucky shirt,' he unbuttons his shirt.

'You are insane!' She whips him with the towel.

He takes her in his arms, 'Where do you think you are going?' He kisses her on her cheeks.

'To take a bath. You must get ready too Mr Ved, since you are taking me out for dinner,' she releases herself.

Angira opens her handbag and eagerly searches inside for something. Ved has other plans. He pulls her back onto the bed and holds her tightly his arms.

'O-o, my stomach,' she screams jovially. 'What are you doing, Ved?'

'Come in my arms,' he grabs her in his arms and rolls down in bed.

'Let me go!'

'Not today,' he kisses her gently. 'What are you thinking?'

'Nothing,' Angira smiles.

She wishes to forget the nightmare she has had to live through in the last few weeks and wishes to spend her time with Ved without any distractions.

'By the way, I have something for you,' she says, surprising Ved.

'Oh really, what is that?' he looks at her with affection.

'So, you won't let me go take a bath?' Angira repeats.

'You look sexier when you are dirty,' he slowly tickles her navel.

'Oh please, it's too cheesy a line,' she tries to release herself and when she can't, she surrenders, throwing the towel to the other side of the bed and hugging him tightly.

'Ah, leave me, I want to show you something,' Angira opens her backpack on the bed and takes out a box. Ved releases her, curious as to what could be in that box. His mind is racing with possibilities.

'Is it something related to the email she received?' he wonders. *'Or is*

it something that Arjun or Anushka gave her?'

While she is taking the time to open the long cylindrical box, these unfounded thoughts flood his mind. 'What is it?' he asks.

'Hold on for a minute, you don't have patience. How will you play on the ground?' she says like an expert.

Girls always have an advice on everything for everyone.

'I am confident on the field, not like the game I played when you came to watch.' Ved still remembers how arrogantly he played and lost the game when Angira came to watch his match for the first time. That was an embarrassing moment for him.

'Great things take a little time,' she says smiling.

'Now, don't be like Arjun,' Ved knows who speaks like this all the time.

Laughing out loud, she says, 'You know that?'

'I know him all too well,' Ved replies.

'But I like his thoughts and opinions on things,' opening the box, she takes out a bottle from it.

'So do I. We had quite a few arguments over the call. I am waiting to see how he will respond when we meet. Now, don't distract me and tell me what's in this bottle,' he asks, sitting up to inspect the bottle properly.

She sits comfortably on the bed, adjusting herself in Ved's arms. He is holding her from the back and his chin is resting on her shoulder. He gently runs his fingers over her neck. She looks at him from the side and kisses him on his cheek.

'By the way, before opening this you need to follow these steps,' pointing to the note hanging from the neck of the bottle.

'Is this some kind of precautionary warning?' Ved enquires.

The bottle has hundreds of small colourful thermocol balls and a message on a scroll tied to it with a red ribbon. It is capped with a golden fabric which is tied-up with the same red ribbon.

He holds the note that is hand-made. He starts reading it:

> We both enjoyed drinks at many occasions; we kissed passionately after drinking and shared the same bed. We had many colourful moments. Today, I am giving you this empty

> bottle with a few words, and I hope you accept it. These colourful small balls signify those moments we shared and a special message that you can't open right now. So keep it safely and wait for the special moment. I know it's tough but the wait adds to the pleasure ;). Maybe I'll ask you to open this on our first wedding night. I love you.

'I love you too,' he grabs her tightly. 'But it's not fair that you won't let me open it.'

'There should be something interesting on our first night after wedding. So you will have to wait patiently until we get married,' she says, winking at him.

'You don't have to worry about that. There are many things we can do to make our nights interesting and exciting,' he turns her on the bed.

'Oh, really?' she asks.

'This man is a player, both on and off ground.'

'That's impressive, but I want your trust and belief; your love, care and respect; I want more thrilling and exciting acts of love,' Angira says, looking serious.

Ved takes the conversation ahead, 'Would you allow me to show my skills?'

Now they are sitting face to face holding hands. Ved presses her lips with his thumb. Angira cannot control her feelings any longer.

'Is this thrill really required?' she asks.

'Yes, I like to try new and different things. Have you ever dreamt of kissing someone wildly?' Ved asks. Angira is looking at the table clock. It shows 5.55 p.m.

'Hey, hey, make a wish! It's 5.55!' Angira suddenly tells him.

'Why, what is that? You are so crazy.'

'Make a wish, make a wish; it's all five in a series.'

He pretends to make a wish, because he doesn't believe in these things. Maybe he has saved his wishes for another day. However, Angira wishes for something and pretends as if she hasn't.

'Someone passed a comment when I had once made a similar wish,' he looks at her and reminds her of the day when Angira came to his place and they shared the glass of wine and some chocolate brownie he had made for her.

She is overwhelmed. It happens when people are precious to us; even superstitions that we dismissed earlier draw our attention and belief. Ved reaches over to kiss her.

'No, this won't be an easy task for you. But, this night would be different from others. I promise.'

'You are so confident, hmm?' Ved seems bewildered now.

Angira puts her hands on his cheeks and kisses him.

She reaches for his ear and murmurs, 'By the way, you know what I dream and read in books?' She blows softly into his ear just to tease him.

'Do you know me?' Ved asks.

'You are different from me—your work, your thinking and your passion. It's true I still don't know many things about you, but yes, I do trust that you won't leave me.'

Angira gently releases herself from his arms and lies down on the bed. She looks up, thinking of something. Tilting her head slightly towards Ved, she presses her lips and then closes her eyes.

'What happened,' he murmurs.

She carries on, 'I have missed you so much. I love you more than anything. I don't want to lose you again. It scares me.'

'Are you trying to kiss me?' she asks.

For some moments, Ved doesn't even move. He is lost in her beauty.

'*Should I kiss her?*' Ved thinks, looking at those lips which demand something from him.

He comes close to her to feel her warmth. She remains silent, but her lips are still quivering.

'Don't ever leave me,' she murmurs softly.

'I'm always with you,' he promises her.

'I love you,' she assures him.

'I love you too.'

'Where are you going?' Ved asks her as she crawls out of bed and takes the bottle that Ved had left on the table.

'Angira, come here please. I want to hug you,' Ved doesn't let her go.

'I want you to open this,' she says, holding out the bottle to him.

'But you told me to open this on our first night after the wedding,' Ved says, taking the bottle from her.

She seems sure and a little uncertain at the same time.

'Because it's the right time and I want you to open this,' Angira repeats herself.

'Are you sure?' he asks her.

'Very much,' she smiles.

This day will be remembered by both of them. This is a rare gift. Curious, he begins to unwrap the gift.

'What if she has written something special for me? What's in the letter?'

Ved becomes impatient. As soon as he opens the bottle, the room starts to small of a fragrant perfume.

'You smell like...' Angira was about to say something when she stops and instead says, 'Now I can tell the difference between day and night.'

'Opening your innerwear at night is easier than...' Ved says.

She interrupts and says, 'Yeah, which you take a few seconds to remove...'

Few thermocol balls fall on the bed while he takes the letter out of the bottle. Angira collects them in her palm, and patiently puts them back in the bottle.

I Am Who I Am, When I Am with You

He unties the ribbon, and as the letter rolls open, it gives out an intense fragrance of a rare sweet perfume. The note is written with sparkle, pens. Angira watches him closely as Ved acknowledges her efforts with a smile. He starts reading the letter.

To,
The most adorable and important person in my life,

Today is the most special day for us. I always wanted to love someone profoundly and you have given me the reason to do so.

I am not creative enough to give surprises like you do, but I always wanted to give you a precious and endearing gift since the day I fell in love with you. As the best things take time to come, I believe the time has come when I want to say something more.

This letter means a lot to me and this is the best way I found to surprise you.

You know when the first time I had gone through a heartbreak, it made me lose all hope about finding love again. I had started to feel as if I was good for nothing.

I don't want to call it my second love, but when you came into my life, you taught me how to hope again. After meeting you, I realized that my second love is the person who will remain with me till the end of my life. You made Arjun's words, about my past having no relevance in my future, come true. It was difficult for me, to trust anyone before you came into my life. Now I understand that falling in love again is better than anything else in the world. It is true that losing someone

makes one vulnerable, but it also makes one stronger.
Everything seems possible when I am with you. In fact, I am me, the real me, when I am with you.
It is said that a girl belongs to another home as she has to leave everything—her family, friends and many more things—once she is married. However, all she carries are her memories, to begin a new chapter in her life.
With you by my side, I don't wish to forget my family, friends and others, but yes, I want to grow old with you.
It is known that first love is about overwhelming emotions. The second tests our maturity. The third, however, is always a compromise.
Make me your second love, but also the last one, because with you I want to be my real self.
And I want you to love me tonight with no barriers, no boundaries.

Ved doesn't say a word and takes her into his arms.

'What are you doing?' she says, laughing and shouting at the same time.

'Just executing your wishes and making the most of tonight,' he says, feeling blissful.

'What are my wishes?' she asks randomly, just to take his attention away from the mischievous things she had mentioned in the letter.

'Let me tell you with my actions.'

'Don't get turned on, I was suppose to take a bath and you...' she gets up.

Ved pulls her back into the bed.

'Let me go, after my bath...' Angira doesn't complete her words, but her eyes convey her wishes.

Ved holds her hand.

'Leave me.'

'No.'

'Let me go.'

'No.'

'Please...'

'No.'

She gives up and kisses him. Their eyes meet, and they are transported to another world.

She gets on top of him and runs her hand over his chest, kissing him passionately.

'Are you wild?' Ved asks.

'Be quiet,' Angira says as Ved slowly kisses her neck.

He knows he is living a dream with open eyes.

'Baby, go down,' he mumbles.

'Wait! Let me love you,' she utters softly.

Ved is running his hand through her hair. He has never felt this before.

'Go down.'

'Hmm...'

They have done this before, but having been apart for so long sparks intense passion and love between them.

'I have never done that before,' she says, looking at him once more. 'First close the window.'

'Okay,' Ved gets up to close the window and draw the curtains. The room is a little darker now. Ved comes back to bed and on his way takes something out from his bag and puts it under the pillow before Angira can see it. Angira moves aside and he lies down next to her. They hug each other and then Ved pulls up her shirt a little bit.

'Remove this,' Ved says.

Angira raises her hands and he takes her shirt off and throws it to the other side of the bed. Ved reaches down her thighs and with his every kiss on her body, she feels ecstatic and is not afraid to show it. Ved runs his hand down her stomach and she grips his hand tightly.

'No, Ved...'

'Remove this.' Ved pulls down her pant as she opens the buttons and unzips it. He then unhooks her bra. She looks conscious and nervous, and stops.

'What are you doing?'

Ved doesn't speak and releases her.

Angira removes his shirt as he goes down on her. Unable to control her excitement, she sits on him and starts kissing his chest. It seems she has taken the reins and Ved is just mesmerized and spellbound watching this new side of her. He can't wait any longer and pulls her down onto the bed. She tries to push his hand away but surrenders to his will. His hand reaches under the pillow.

'What are you doing?'

Ved doesn't respond and takes out the condom from under the pillow.

'No,' she says, easily guessing what it is. 'We're not going to do this. I am nervous. This is not the right time.'

'I am not going to have sex,' Ved says, holding the condom in his hand.

'Then what are you going to do with it?' she asks him.

'Last time, I had wet your clothes and your bed too. So this is just to keep everything clean and clear,' he gives it to her.

'Okay,' she takes it and tears the pack with her teeth.

Ved wants to use it because they are both on the edge and he wants to be prepared.

'You are crazy, you know that?,' Angira spanks him.

He ignores it and grabs her bosom. Angira feels like a bride on her honeymoon night. Ved is in seventh heaven. She runs her hand through his hair and kisses his forehead. Ved feels the softness of her body and she closes her eyes. Ved pushes her back on the bed and kisses her softly. They hold each other like this for hours. Angira climbs on Ved, and unfasting her bra entangled around his knees, she goes down on him.

It's time for Ved to turn her around. This time he goes down on her, kissing every inch of her body. He can literally taste the sweetness of this moment. Angira feels a current passing through her body. He can feel her respond to every touch of his. Her toes are tingly, their heart rate is really high, and they can't focus on anything other than the sensations that are rushing through their bodies. He takes control and starts stroking till her last moan. She gives her best by locking him in her legs. She is wild now, and doesn't let him stop. She is warm and covered in sweat. All of a sudden his muscles relaxed and then he feels too sensitive to be touched anymore. They cuddle for some time in bed.

'I don't want to go,' confesses Ved.

'Hey listen, why don't you move in with me?'

'Meaning?' Ved is confused.

'You can move in. There is enough space for both of us. Anyway, Charu and I are the only ones who live there,' Angira says with assurance.

'Yes, you have Charu to talk to and I have Arjun.'

'Yes, but she lives in her room. She won't get disturbed if you come. We'll manage,' Angira persists. 'I had told Charu a few days ago about this and she had agreed to it. In fact, she was happy about the idea, but shit happened and then...'

'But what reason will I give Arjun for moving in with you. And what if he tells Anushka. Your mom will transport me to hell.'

Lying in bed, they try to figure a way out.

Angira remembers the lines Arjun had told her about love.

Love makes you happy,
Love makes you weak,
That's the beauty of it,
Sometimes it floats, sometimes it's deep.

After spending an unforgettable night with each other, they leave for Mumbai next morning. On their way suddenly something strikes him and he gets up to open his laptop. He opens his Gmail account once again.

'What happened?' Angira asks him.

'Just checking something,' he says, trying hard to figure out.

He goes to the following navigation of Gmail > Settings > Forwarding and POP/IMAP > Forwarding, and finds the email ID of Iona D'souza.

Ved had never imagined that Iona could go to such an extent.

'What happened? What's that?' Angira asks him, trying to understand the situation.

'She was stalking me. I still can't believe it,' Ved holds his head and closes his eyes.

He wonders how she could do this. She was stalking him even when they were just friends.

'What?' Angira is shocked looking at the screen.

'But how?' she wants to know more.

How can Iona be so possessive to keep a track of his activities? Ved recalls each and every moment from their past when he shared his Gmail account with Iona. He remembers that one day during vacations they were at their respective homes, and had planned to do a video chat on Gmail. He gave his Gmail password to her so that she could install a webcam and resolve the issue as he was busy working on something and Iona wanted to talk to him desperately. Iona had logged into his account and installed the webcam after which they spoke happily that day. But her possessiveness took a dangerous turn and she started stalking him. She never wanted to lose him, so she did this.

'Ved, how can she do that?' Angira is too angry.

'Yes, see. She put her email id and then verified it, so that afterwards even if I changed the password or did anything on my Gmail account, she received a carbon copy of my activities on her email id,' Ved shows Angira the evidence.

Ved feels weak and cheated. He removed her email id and does not tell Iona anything. He regains composure and tells Angira not to share this news with anyone, not even Arjun, Anushka or Charu.

He Said, She Said, We Said

There are so many reasons to party. Ved and Angira have moved in together and he is going to Kolkata to play for the city. Anushka will be told about the development soon and he will personally ask Angira's mom for her hand the next time he meets her. Arjun and Ved have cleared all the doubts that had fogged their heads and their friendship. They understand each other better now and are happy for one another. Every day they relive their college days together, with Anushka in tow.

Tonight Angira has thrown a party at a restaurant for everyone to celebrate all this and much more. Ved too wants to celebrate the time spent in the apartment where he fell in love with Angira, before they begin a new life together.

The surprise element in the party was the presence of Anushka and Iona, which was not expected. Angira sits on the extreme left with Charu, and Arjun is on the extreme right on the red-and-white sofa with fancy cushions. Anushka and Iona are crammed in between them, and Ved sits in front of them on a single sofa. It's easy for them to make fun of him today.

'You are sitting at the right place,' Iona says, looking at Ved.

Ved doesn't speak.

Elder siblings play a huge role in cementing a relationship. Anushka is happy for her sister and for Ved, whom she likes a lot. She knows convincing her parents will be difficult, but it is doable. Ved has learnt a few tricks to impress their parents and Anushka is confident that their marriage is imminent. Soon Ved will be in Delhi to speak to Anushka's family and all will be settled.

'No, I'd rather have Arjun sitting here,' Ved says, getting up from the chair.

'Don't be so kind, today's your day. I give it to you as you have become a sensible man,' Arjun says with a smile.

'Don't do that, he deserves this day today,' Anushka defends Ved with a sharp laugh.

'He just got selected. It's not like he has won the match,' Charu jumps into the conversation and then realizes that she should not criticize him.

'Yes, he has just been selected, but he will definitely win the match. He has to,' Angira says with affection.

Arjun takes a glass of water; Iona picks up a menu card and says, 'I need to stuff myself with food.'

She asks Angira to order something good. Anushka and Arjun are talking while Ved is just staring away, intensely thinking about something. Charu has been noticing him for the last few minutes.

'So how's everything at your end?' Arjun asks Iona.

'Life is good. The next trip is to Paris,' Iona looks happy and cheerful answering him.

It was her dream to visit the French capital. Iona will be in Mumbai for a few more days before heading to her dream destination.

'That's great,' he congratulates her.

'So what will you have?' Iona asks him, checking the menu card.

Arjun passes the menu card to others because he isn't sure what to order.

'We don't know,' Ved says suddenly.

'What don't you know?' Charu asks him.

'Just order what you want,' responds Ved.

'I'll have Mint with a Hole,' Iona mentions.

'I'll have End of the Road,' Anushka adds.

And Angira orders I Clove You, a whiskey-based shot with a strong taste of clove. Arjun places his order as well.

They are enjoying in each other's company.

'Well, listen...listen up guys,' Arjun announces. 'Do we really know why we are here today?'

'Of course, the future star...' Charu starts sniggering and others follow her.

'Apart from that, on this day four months ago, Ved took Angira on their first date. It's their four-month anniversary, you guys!'

Everyone congratulates them. Angira is just stunned.

'You remember that?' Ved asks him, pleasantly surprised.

'Yes, I do. You told me...'

'But you are really bad with the dates Arjun. You forgot my birthday,' Anushka says, punching him jestily on his arms.

'That's because I wanted to be the last to wish you so that you remember it forever,' Arjun replies with a naughty smile. 'So, congratulations to both of you. Keep smiling and keep rocking!'

Everyone claps for the lovely couple and wishes them for their new beginning. Angira looks at Arjun and passes a smile without exchanging any words. Anushka raises her glass and asks everyone to drink their shot.

'Yeah,' Charu picks up her glass and orders the others to do the same.

'1...2...3,' Iona counts and the alcohol slips down everyone's throat.

'Thanks,' Angira smiles.

'You have already thanked me enough,' Arjun says.

'One more time...'

'Then one more time, may I say congratulations to you.'

'By the way, how did you remember the date?' she asks with a sense of curiosity.

'I set reminders for important dates. Now don't tell anyone,' Arjun says, raising his eyebrows and placing a finger on his lips.

'Are you serious?' She shakes her head.

After a few hours, everyone seems to be in high spirits.

'I want one more,' Angira declares her intention to drink while Arjun, Ved and Anushka talk.

'I want one more too,' Iona calls out.

Arjun looks at Anushka, who tries to keep Angira busy with potato swirls so that she does not ask for another drink.

'Angira, you shouldn't have any more drinks. You've already had three back to back,' Anushka says.

Iona looks at her and seems to be thinking something.

'When did you order this?' Anushka asks her.

Iona had ordered a large drink of vodka when everyone was busy chit-chatting.

'Just wanted to have...' Iona mumbles.

Angira remembers something while Anushka is talking to Iona.

'Let's play a game. I am sure everyone will enjoy this,' Angira says excitedly.

'What game are you talking about?' Iona asks her.

'Please don't bore us,' Charu warns her.

'No, it's fun. I promise,' Angira says confidently.

'So what's the game?' Ved asks curiously.

'Actually, it's called flip, sip or strip, but we are not going to strip. The rule of the game is, someone will flip a coin and while the coin is in the air, one person will call heads or tails. If that person guesses it right, then the coin is passed onto the person on the right, and if he or she guesses it wrong, then the coin is passed on to the person on the left. The twist is, if your guess is wrong, you need to drink a shot. Just to make sure things don't go out of hand, you can't sip more than twice in a row,' Angira explains it well and takes charge of the game.

Flip, Sip and the Stripping of Truth!

'No, you guys need to go home as well, no more drinks,' Arjun tells them.

He is worried about dropping everyone home safely, as always.

'It's fun, let's have some more shots,' Angira pleads.

Arjun rarely says a no to Angira because being her bestfriend, he always gives her the space that she deserves. Today she has all the rights.

'But we'll play just one round,' Arjun says.

They order some drinks and the game starts with Angira. Ved flips the coin.

'Heads,' Angira calls.

'It's tails,' Ved says and everyone hoots.

Angira downs the shot, but cringes a little as she doesn't like its taste. Despite that she finishes the drink in one go. She then passes the coin to the left where Iona is sitting.

'It's heads,' Iona says and it turns out to be the wrong guess.

Iona takes the shot, though she is already quite drunk. Iona passes the coin to Charu who is sitting on her left. Charu's guess is right and again the turn comes back to Iona. Iona's guess is wrong again and she drinks another shot. Thanks to the wrong guesses, Ved and Iona are the ones who have consumed more alcohol than the others.

They are drunk out of their minds and are enjoying every bit of it. Suddenly something flashes in Ved's mind. He stops drinking and instead drinks a glass of water. The game goes on and almost everyone takes at least one shot, except Anushka. Time flies and it is 10.45 p.m. Ved wanted to clear things with Iona, but the situation does not seem favourable. Iona is drunk. Anushka is talking to Arjun, telling him that he needs to drop Iona at her friend's place as Iona is in no condition to travel alone. Anushka and Iona had come directly to the party to give the couple a surprise, but now, Ved tries to recollect if he left anything unmanaged at Angira's place.

'Anushka shouldn't come to know that I am staying with Angira. What if she finds my shoes over there? Did I hide it before leaving? Shit!!! I left my innerwear in the laundry basket,' he panics.

Ved looks worried now. He takes her phone out and messages Angira on WhatsApp about the situation. Angira looks serious too and they both have the same expression. She messages him back.

What do we do now?

Ved replies while Arjun notices that they are busy chatting on WhatsApp.

I don't know.

Do one thing, drop us at our place.
You talk to Anushka downstairs.
I'll go upstairs and clean the rooms.

Confused and worried Ved texts her.

Can you do this?

Yes, I can.
You just talk about whatever you want. Talk about football, Delhi, Mumbai whatever comes in your mind, but keep her busy.

If she finds your innerwear at my place, she will surely take me back to Delhi.

Ok, put everything in the bag and keep it under the bed.
Don't forget to hide the things which are under the pillow :P

Didn't you throw that?

I threw the used one in the dustbin; the unused one is still under the pillow.

Now, dance...

LOL

Charu gets up, saying, 'Excuse me.'

Angira and Ved, now conscious of having been on their phones for too long, look at her.

'What happened?' Anushka utters.

With the same tenor, Charu says, 'Washroom...'

'Okay,' Anushka says.

Iona also gets up and tails her.

Arjun keeps an eye on Charu while the girls go to the washroom. Arjun looks at Ved and says something in gestures, something that Anushka doesn't understand. Angira wants to talk to Iona, but Arjun and Ved stop her. With everyone in good mood, Ved doesn't want to ruin the moment by asking Iona why she tried to mess with him.

'Let's go to the dance floor,' Angira says.

Although everyone's enjoying, there is Angira who parties like there's no tomorrow.

'It's already 11.45,' Anushka says.

'We still have an hour,' Angira reminds her.

Ved looks excited to take her to the dance floor, but in front of Anushka he doesn't speak much. Angira makes them dance as they await Charu and Iona to join them. Ved books their cabs for 12.45 a.m. as 1 a.m. is the closing time.

'Let's go now,' Angira says, standing up as Charu returns.

'Where is Iona?' Arjun asks, disconnecting the call.

'No idea. Let me call her,' Angira dials her number.

Everyone is worried for Iona.

'Though she can control herself even after multiple drinks, Arjun, could you please look in there?' Angira says, pointing towards the washroom.

Arjun nods and Ved also gets up.

'She is coming,' Anushka informs them.

Iona waves from the other end, walking towards them.

'Let's go,' says Angira, coming upto Ved.

Iona is totally drunk as she reaches for the sofa where everyone is sitting.

'Iona, are you okay?' Anushka asks her and helps her sit on the sofa.

'I am fine, I am fine,' she says.

'No, you are not,' Anushka says, again trying to make her sit comfortably.

'I am perfectly fine!' She laughs aloud.

People sitting next to them stare at her.

'Yes, I can see that. Iona you are not in your senses. Sit down. We'll leave in some time,' Anushka speaks, offering her a glass of water.

'Okay, we'll head home,' Charu decides.

She wanted to dance, but with Iona drunk out of her mind the timing couldn't have been worse.

'No, I am fine,' Iona says.

'You look like an obnoxious drunkard,' Charu says.

'You also had the same amount as me. I just had a few extra shots,' she replies. 'By the way, before we leave, I want to say something.'

There is a sense of seriousness on her face.

'Iona, it's getting very late,' Arjun says.

'I'll take just five minutes of your time,' she says.

She looks like she has prepared a speech and is nervous before going on the dais.

'What do you want to say?' Arjun asks as Ved, Anushka and Angira come closer.

Arjun is clearly impatient now. Ved is in his own world, constantly thinking of how to get out of trouble with Anushka.

Iona starts, 'Many congratulations to your success and I pray you achieve more and more success. You've got what you wanted in your life—your passion and your partner to walk with you. Forever and forever.'

Iona continues, 'I wish you'll continue to strive for excellence as you have done so far. I really appreciate you for what you have achieved in life till now and we all are proud of you. I wish you greater success in future and hope that you, as a sportsperson, add to the glory of the game and to us.'

Everyone claps and congratulates Ved once again.

She adds, while others are still clapping, pointing towards Ved, 'I have known him for six years now...'

Everyone is shocked, except Ved and Arjun.

Ved looks at Arjun and considers interrupting her before she says anything else. That garba night, that email, those moments he spent with her. Arjun stops him. But Ved is upset; he is drunk and cannot control himself from speaking up.

'Before you congratulate me, I have a few questions for you,' Ved comes closer to Iona.

'What happened?' Iona looks a little uncomfortable because in the years she has known Ved, he has never expressed himself like this.

Ved comes in front of her and is about to slap her, but controls himself, tightening his fists in anger.

Everyone is shocked.

Arjun tries to control Ved.

'No, let me show her what I am!' Ved shouts. 'You can't imagine.'

Arjun pulls Ved away as people are staring at them. Everybody is dumbstruck.

'Never show me your face, and this time don't even try to follow me, Iona. Consider this a suggestion and a warning,' Ved yells at Iona.

There is a hint of regret on her face, but now, it's too late.

'What the fuck?' Charu cannot understand what just happened.

Anushka tries to control him. Others are just stunned and won't look away.

'Ved, you are not in your senses,' Arjun tries to normalize the situation.

Iona starts crying. Anushka comes closer to her as she is standing alone. Ved warns Anushka.

'Anushka. No, Arjun leave me. I have a few questions to ask her,' Ved releases himself from Arjun's grip.

'Ved, you are drunk,' Arjun knows things are getting worse.

'Arjun!!' Ved shouts and continues, 'No, I am not drunk. I was drunk that day. I was drunk at the garba night when she ruined everything in my life.'

'Ved, whatever has happened was my mistake. Now please don't make a scene over here. We can talk calmly,' Iona feels alone, though Anushka is standing by her side.

'Calmly? What's that,' Ved asks her, maintaining the same pitch.

He looks at her like never before. 'Do you remember what happened four years ago in college? It was me who had fallen for you and left everything for you. I loved you, but you filed a case against me. Look at them. These were my friends who saved me from that situation. I fought with them because I never wanted to leave you. I begged you but you still ruined my life. You never cared for me. Why did you do that? I always treated you well and yet again you have tried to ruin things for me.'

Iona is afraid. 'But we had resolved that it was in the past. We were in college that time. I have apologized to you several times for that. How many times do I have to say sorry to you?'

'Sorry? Oh really. Should I leave her and come along with you? You who never cared about friendship and couldn't respect love. Do you even know what love is? Do you really know what friendship is? Do you even care about them? These are my friends, my world. Iona, it has taken years for me to come to this place where I'm finally happy. Don't try to create any problems for us.'

'Ved, it's enough. Let's go,' Arjun holds his hand.

Arjun is in tears. He does not know what to say anymore. He understands what Ved has gone through over the years. He comes to Ved, who hugs him tightly, 'I am sorry.'

He bursts into tears.

'It's okay,' Arjun says, breaking down.

Anushka reaches for them and puts her hand on Ved's shoulder.

'Because of me, you both have suffered in college and even after college,' Ved hugs both of them tightly.

'I am always with you, Ved,' Arjun doesn't want to speak any further because then he too would not be able to stop his tears.

'Please don't cry. We are with you.' Anushka holds Arjun's hand tightly and closes her eyes.

'Everyone left me in college. I was alone. Nobody talked to me. I wanted to tell people that I wasn't wrong, but nobody trusted me. Even my juniors were not talking to me,' Ved is crying because he has suffered for years for no fault of his own.

'I know, Ved. Please don't cry,' Arjun pats him.

'It's okay.' Anushka keeps her hand on his head.

'Don't cry.' Arjun pulls his chin up and looks at him and says, 'You are a football player. They don't cry, hmm…now you have said what you wanted to say,' Arjun can't stop his tears anymore.

Arjun hugs him back tightly and says, with tears in his eyes, 'Everyone has to pay their dues. Let's forget whatever happened.'

'Now everything is fine. No more tears. We are with you,' Anushka says.

Angira comes from the back, and trying to join the group hug, says, 'Please include me in your circle. I am the newcomer in this group.'

Ved hugs her, 'I love you. Thanks for coming into my life.'

'I love you too. Now, don't cry. So, are you guys including me in your group?'

Arjun and Anushka look at each other and then at them, smiling. They are happy as they hold eachother's hands.

'Yes, welcome to The AAVA Group!'

The friendship which was broken four years ago in college is renewed now with a lot more trust and love.

When the cabs arrive, Charu decides to drop Iona off.

Suddenly, Arjun receives a call from his mom.

'Mom, what happened? Why have you called so late?'

'Arjun, actually your dad and I went to a marriage party thrown by Mishra uncle.'

'Who is Mishra uncle?' Arjun asks confused.

'The one who works with your dad. His brother's daughter is pursuing BDS (Bachelor of Dental Surgery) and is looking for a good match. So he asked me if you can come during Diwali holidays and meet her. I saw her picture and she looks beautiful. I'll WhatsApp you the details.'

'Mom, do you know what time it is. It's 12.55 in the night and you're calling me...'

'I thought you would be awake,' she says.

Angira, Anushka and Ved laugh together.

'Let's go,' Arjun says and then they leave. While in the cab, Angira, Ved and Anushka write something on a sticky note and give it to Arjun.

It says:

The past is not our future.

I believe.

I believe.

I believe.

Epilogue

I smile as I look at the sticky note Angira had given me the night we settled everything between us. I have kept it in my wallet since then and read it several times a day. It makes me smile and the simplicity of the lines always makes me wonder about life.

The past is not our future.

I am lucky to have friends like them who mean the world to me. I can call them in the middle of the night. They fight with me for the last bits of food. They demand a huge bribe when I ask them for help and they make me laugh when I am low and distressed. They make me realize that not everything has to be perfect, that I will make mistakes and whatever has happened has happened for the best.

Over the last few days I have wondered about the mysteries of life. There is always this urge to make things happen. To work hard in order to achieve our dreams. Sometimes when these dreams come true, we feel as if it was not us who achieved them. This disbelief turns into courage to make other dreams come true, thanks to the people in our lives. For me my friends, family and well-wishers are everything.

I wonder sometimes why I keep the note with me. Though all the answers are yet to be found, one must be grateful for what one has.

I message Anushka.

'Can you please call her soon?' I ask the lady at the reception of The Publication's office.

'Sir, Neha is on the way.'

Anushka enters the reception and smiles as she sits by my side. Anushka and Neha are people who have helped me grow and have seen every dimension of me. Ved rightly says that one should never leave people who know your secrets.

'You are late, Anushka.'

'You can wait for me, right?'

I will always wait for her. She has stood up for me every time.

'I am a little nervous, Anushka,' I say.

'This is not an interview. Relax.'

Neha finally arrives at the reception.

'Sorry to have kept you guys waiting. Ready?'

'I won't say I'm alright with it,' I smile indulgently.

'Would you like some coffee or tea?' she asks us with a smile.

'Nah! We're good,' I reply.

'Then should we begin?' she asks, looking at the bunch of printouts in my hand.

'Looking good,' I say.

'Pretty is the right word,' Neha laughs at her own words.

'Never marry a girl who is an editor. She'll keep finding mistakes in your words,' I declare with satisfaction.

'Every girl has this quality. By the way, when will you marry Anushka? You guys are so cute together.'

'We're just good friends,' I reply, a little embarrassed.

'Ah! Alright.'

While I am writing for the third time, I will tell the story to a bunch of unknown faces first and then submit it to my editor. At the cafeteria, we are welcomed by seven people which makes me feel nervous and excited at the same time. They form a semi- circle around me and listen to me with rapt attention. Anushka, Angira and Ved stand behind me. Charu is running late. Quite normal for her.

'Firstly, I would like to introduce the people who have made it possible for me to be here,' I smile looking at everyone. 'These are the people who pushed me hard to help me become who I am today.'

'Who is your favourite in the story?' Ved asks me.

'Each one of us is incomplete without the other. I am not answering that question.'

Before I began, Ved, Angira and Charu leave me after wishing me luck with Charu. Angira is introducing Ved to her mom. It is their big day. Anushka stays with me to listen to the story one more time.

'We need to wish this man some luck. He is going to ask for his girlfriend's hand.'

While Ved and Angira blush, they are flooded with enthusiastic wishes. Once they leave, I continue with my story of love, friendship, affection and a little infatuation.

Once the story is done, I realize I was in a trance. Neha sits next to me and keeps staring at me.

'I am done,' I smile.

After she gives me her inputs on the story, we eat lunch at the cafeteria.

'So when do I need to submit the book?' I ask Neha.

'Tell me something about the character Arjun,' Neha asks me.

'Do you really want to know? You'll laugh at him.'

'Whatever, now go ahead...'

'Well, Arjun...he is someone who believes in love and thinks it exists. He believes that the best things take time to come in one's life. He has come from nothing and now he has something. One day he'll have everything and that will be because of his friends and the relationships he has built over the years. He stands up for his friends through thick and thin; that's what makes him special,' I say proudly. 'Those are the people who helped him overcome so much in his past. They taught him that the future has little to do with the past.'

'I could easily guess that that Arjun is you, but why don't you reveal it to your readers,' Neha probes further.

'Because I don't want people to read my story. I want them to read a story of love, commitment and friendship that fits together in one sheath.'

'That's a nice thought.'

'I'll send the manuscript next week.'

'Thanks Anuj, it was nice meeting you. Keep coming back.' Neha waves us goodbye outside The Publication's office.

Nanu and Ma surprise me at the exit.

'What are you guys doing here?'

'Hello Nanu, hello Aunty,' Anushka greets them.

'Angira called me and informed that you guys are here,' Nanu says.

Anushka and I look at each other in confusion.

'Now you'll surely get your answer,' I whisper to Neha, who is still standing at the exit.

'Let's go,' my mom says.

'Where?' I ask her.

'Anushka's home,' Nanu responds to my question happily and continues muttering into my ears, 'Let the friendship become something a little more long-lasting.'

'Mom...okay, meet Anushka. Anushka this is my mom and Nanu,' I introduce them.

Neha smiles as we leave. She has got the answer she was looking for.

Acknowledgements

This is the last, but one of my favourite sections, where I can write anything I feel like. Here, I get a chance to speak for those who mean a lot to me.

I never went to playschool. I didn't study in a convent school because my education mostly comprised the values, culture and tradition that our forefathers passed onto the next generation. These teachings were modified with time by my supportive family and imparted to me throughout my life. My grandfather used to say that the biggest success is to make people happy with your presence, to understand them and listen to them when nobody is there for them. To stand with them when the rest of the world is against them, is what's most important. That is when you will not need monetary happiness because you will have more than what you ever dreamed of in your life. That time will give you immense pleasure to live life.

He was right.

Writing was not part of my life. It just happened in my life because when something burns inside, it leaves some smoke and perhaps a fire to prove oneself. In college, before giving my first corporate interview, I was told, look at your weaknesses as your strength and then see the magic. My weakness was my past. I lived and then found my strength through my writing, which I always wanted to convey to others, that true love and friendship still exists if you have good people around.

Before I become any more sentimental, my heartfelt and genuine thanks to all the names I've mentioned here. I'll forever be grateful to you all for taking me ahead in the journey of writing this tale of my life. This time the list has become a little longer.

Thanks to the whole team of Rupa Publications for discussing and answering my crazy questions.

Ved and Angira, the craziest couple I have ever seen in my life, who made it possible and gave me the spark to write their story, which surely changed my view of how to live my life. Charu, thanks for being a part of it and for the support.

Iona, I don't know what she is doing these days as she has changed her number and does not appear on social media either. I hope she will be back on time to wish Ved and Angira before they become parents.

To all those classmates and college students, who left us because Ved was involved in a rape attempt case. For your information, no, he wasn't.

To my corporate team of Bay46, Mumbai. Their presence has been absolutely fabulous. I am the craziest person when I am with them.

Mayank, Ankit and Ankur, thanks for being with me from the day I used to ring your doorbell to go for tuition classes.

Sneha Panday, for standing by me, with whom I spent the most wonderful time.

I am not mentioning any more names because everyone who is connected to me, whether on Facebook, Twitter or offline, is precious for me. So I thank them, as they all are my extended family.

I love my family for watching over me and for listening to me always—for the support that went beyond this book. Moreover, thanks to all those who unflinchingly gave me their hand to hold. They are the ones who read the book, sitting together like school kids.

In addition, those who criticized me, pulled me back and kicked me out of their lives in my toughest times, I want to say thanks to them. Somewhere they gave me the courage and passion to go ahead in life.

A lot of love to the cities I spent a few years of my life in—

Bareilly: For bringing me up with affection and helping me learn how to be happy with the small things in life.

Lucknow: For always treating me like its own son and giving me so much love.

Kanpur: Where I spent a year of my life and learnt about friendship.

Guna: The place that made me an engineer and a narrator of my own life, and for those treasured memories of college days.

Delhi: This place gave me memories to remember for the rest of my life.

Mumbai: It is known as the city where people come to fulfil their dreams, and I know it to be true.

Bangalore: The city of lovely, romantic weather and wonderful people. I thank you for the lovely time.

Kolkata: Last, but definitely not the least, thanks to Kolkata for appreciating my writing and giving me so much love.

I intentionally write about my readers in the end so that I can end the book with my appreciation for them. You were always my strength. I always intend to write true stories which happen around me and inspire me to write. After all, why should I write fiction when there are so many real stories around me. Warm thanks to all my readers, those who are connected to me on social media, as well as those who are not. You all mean a lot to me; I try my best to answer your messages and mails. So, stay connected. Keep smiling. Love you all.

Facebook: www.facebook.com/anujtiwari.official
Email: anujtiwari.official@gmail.com
Twitter: @AnujOfficial